D0414568

MISSING

CREATIVE
COMMUNITY DAY

Loughborough University

This book was shared at Loughborough University's
<u>**Creative Community Day 2019**</u>
When you've finished, please pass it on to someone who might enjoy it too!
We'd love to know where this book travels, tweet us **@LboroSCL**

Look out for more titles
in the MISSING series

When Lightning Strikes
Code Name Cassandra
Safe House
Sanctuary

MISSING

Missing You

Meg Cabot

Writing as Jenny Carroll

SIMON AND SCHUSTER

Many thanks to Jennifer Brown, John Henry Dreyfuss, Laura Langlie, Amanda Maciel, Abby McAden, and Ingrid van der Leeden.

SIMON & SCHUSTER
First published in Great Britain in 2007 by Simon & Schuster UK Ltd.
Africa House, 64–78 Kingsway, London WC2B 6AH
A CBS COMPANY

Originally published in the USA in 2006 by HarperTempest,
an imprint of HarperCollins Publishers, New York.

Copyright © 2006 by Meg Cabot, LLC.
Cover illustration copyright © by Nicola Cramp, 2007
All Rights Reserved.

A CIP catalogue record for this book is available
from the British Library upon request.

This book is a work of fiction. Names, characters, places and
incidents are either a product of the author's imagination or are
used fictitiously. Any resemblance to actual people living or dead,
events or locales is entirely coincidental.

ISBN-10: 1-41691-052-2
ISBN-13: 978-1-41691-052-7

1 3 5 7 9 10 8 6 4 2

Printed and bound in Great Britain by
CPI Bath

For all the readers who asked for it

CHAPTER

1

My name is Jessica Mastriani.

You might have heard of me. It's fine with me if you haven't, though. In fact, I kind of prefer it that way.

The reason you might have heard of me is that I'm the one the press kept calling "Lightning Girl," because I got struck by lightning a few years ago and developed this so-called psychic power to find missing people in my dreams.

It was this very big deal at the time. At least in Indiana, which is where I'm from. There was even a TV show about me, based on my life. It wasn't EXACTLY based on my life. I mean, they made a lot of stuff up. Like about me going to Quantico to train as an FBI agent. That never happened. Oh, and they killed off my dad on the show, too. In real life, he's actually alive and well.

But I didn't mind (though my dad wasn't too happy about it) because they still had to pay me. For the right to use my name and my story and all of that. It ended up being quite a lot of money, even though the show is only on cable, not even one of the main networks.

My parents take the checks I get every month and invest them for me. I haven't even had to touch the capital yet. I just spend a little bit of the interest now and then, like when I run short on cash for food or the rent or whatever. Which isn't that often lately, because I've got a summer job, and all. Not the world's greatest job or anything. But at least it's not with the FBI, like on the TV show about me.

I did work for the FBI for a while. There was this special division, headed by this guy, Cyrus Krantz. I worked for them for almost a year.

See, it wasn't supposed to go the way it did. My life, I mean. First there was the whole getting struck by lightning thing. That so wasn't in the plans. Not that anyone—anyone sane, anyway—would CHOOSE to get struck by lightning and get psychic powers, because, trust me on this, it completely sucks. I mean, I guess it's all right for the people I helped.

But it was no bed of roses for me, believe me.

Then there was the war. Like the lightning, it just came from out of nowhere. And like the lightning, it changed everything. Not just the fact that suddenly, everyone on our street back in Indiana had an American flag in their front yard, and we were all glued to CNN 24/7. For me, a lot more changed than just that. I mean, I hadn't even finished high school yet, and still, Uncle Sam was all, "I WANT YOU."

And the thing was, they needed me. *Really* needed me. Innocent people were dying. What was I going to do, say no?

Although the truth is, I tried to say no at first. Until my brother Douglas—the one I'd always thought would be the most against my going—was the one who went, "Jess. What are you doing? You *have* to go."

So I went.

At first they said I could work from home. Which was good, because I really needed to finish twelfth grade, and all.

But there were people they needed to find, fast. What was I supposed to do? It was a *war.*

I know to most people, the war was, like, somewhere way over there. Your average American, I bet they didn't even THINK about it, except, you know, when they turned on the news at night and saw people getting blown up and stuff. "This many U.S. Marines were killed today," they'd say on the news. The next day, people heard, "We found this many terrorists hiding in a cave in the hills of Afghanistan."

Well, it wasn't like that for me. I didn't get to see the

war on the news. Instead, I saw it live. Because I was there. I was there because I was the one telling them which of those caves to look in for those people they needed to find so badly.

I tried to do it from home at first, and then later, from Washington.

But a lot of times, when I'd tell them where to go look, they'd go there and then they'd come back and be all, "There's no one there."

But I knew they were wrong. Because I was never wrong. Or I guess I should say my *power* never was.

So finally I was like, "Look, just send me there, and I'll SHOW you."

Some of the people I found, you heard about on the news. Other people I found, they kept secret. Some of the people I found, we couldn't get to, on account of where they were hiding, deep in the mountains. Some of the people I found, they decided just to keep tabs on, and wait it out. Some of the people I found ended up dead.

But I found them. I found them all.

And then the nightmares came. And I couldn't sleep anymore.

Which meant I couldn't find anyone anymore. Because I couldn't dream.

Posttraumatic stress syndrome. Or PTSS. That's

what they called it, anyway. They tried everything they could think of to help me. Drugs. Therapy. A week by a big fancy pool in Dubai. None of it worked. I still couldn't sleep.

So, in the end, they sent me home, thinking maybe I'd get better there, once everything was back to normal again.

The problem with that was, when I got home everything wasn't back to normal. Everything was different.

I guess that's not fair. I guess what it was, was that *I* was different. Not everyone else. I mean, you see stuff like that—kids screaming at you not to take their father, things blowing up . . . *people* blowing up—and you're only seventeen years old, or whatever—hey, even if you're forty—it makes it hard just to come back home a year later, and, like . . . do what? Go to the mall? Get a pedicure? Watch *SpongeBob SquarePants*?

Please.

But I couldn't go back to doing what I'd been doing, either. I mean, for the FBI. I couldn't find *myself*, let alone anyone else. Because I wasn't "Lightning Girl" anymore.

What I was, I was discovering slowly, was something I hadn't been for a long time:

I was normal.

As normal as a girl like me CAN be, anyway. I mean,

I CHOOSE to wear my hair almost as short as some of the marines I worked with.

And I will admit to having a certain affection for hogs. The motorcycle kind. Not the roll-around-in-mud kind.

And I will admit, my idea of a fun day has never been to yak on the phone or instant message my friends, then go see a fun romantic comedy. For one thing, I only have one, maybe two friends. And for another, I like movies where things blow up.

Or at least I used to. Until things around me *actually* started blowing up on a more or less regular basis. Now I like to see movies about cartoon aliens that come to live with little girls in Hawaii, or fish that are lost. That sort of thing.

Other than those few, minor details, though, I'm normal as apple pie. It took a long time, but I did it. Seriously. I have what, by any standards, could be called a normal life. I live in a normal apartment, with a normal roommate. Well, okay, Ruth, my best friend since forever, isn't exactly normal. But she's normal enough. We do normal things, like shop for groceries together, and order in Chinese food, and watch the dumb TV shows she likes so much.

And okay, Ruth tries to get me to go out all the time, like to concerts in the park, or whatever. And me, I'd rather stay home and practice my flute. So maybe that's not so normal.

But hey, she got me my summer job. And it's a pretty normal summer job, in that it pays hardly anything. Isn't that what a normal nineteen-year-old pretty much expects? A summer job that pays hardly anything?

So that's normal. Fortunately, with my pension from the FBI—yeah, I was on salary. I wasn't an agent, or anything. But they had to pay me. Are you kidding? Like I was going to work for them for free?—and the interest from my investments from the TV show, plus what Mom and Dad send from home, I get by fine.

Plus, you know, it's not like I'm out here on my own. Ruth and I split everything, the cost of groceries, the rent—which is pretty high, even though we only have a one bedroom, which we also split. Still, it's in Hell's Kitchen, which, in case you didn't know, is in New York City, the most expensive place to live in the world—everything, down the middle.

Anyway, the job . . . I guess it's cool. It helps kids, which, in a weird way, is what I was doing when I first started out with the whole lightning thing, and all (before I started ruining kids' lives, instead of saving them, by helping to arrest their dads). Ruth got a job at this not-for-profit group. She heard about it off the Summer Employment board at school. She ended up going to Columbia, after being admitted to every single school she applied to.

A lot of people—like Ruth's parents, and her twin brother, Skip, who went to Indiana University, and who is here in New York for the summer, working as an intern at a company down on Wall Street—think Ruth could get a better, more highly paid summer job, considering she goes to Columbia, which is an Ivy League school, and all.

But Ruth's all, "I'm making a difference," which is cool, because she is. What she does is organize musicians and actors and stuff to go around to inner-city day-care centers and camps, and they help the kids put on plays or musicals or whatever, because the city doesn't have enough money to hire actual, certified teachers for this.

At first I thought this was stupid—Ruth's summer job, I mean. What can putting on a play during day camp do for some kid whose mom is a crackhead?

Then one day Ruth forgot her wallet at home and needed me to bring it to her. So I did, even though this put a major cramp in my practicing.

But it ended up being worth it. Because I saw right away that I was wrong. Putting on a play at camp can make a huge difference to a kid, even a kid with serious problems at home (not like having a dad in a U.S.

detention center, but like having a junkie grandma, or whatever). It's pretty cool to see a kid who's never seen a play before suddenly ACTING in one. Or—which is the part where I come in—a kid who's never played a musical instrument suddenly PLAYING one.

And it's cool for me, too, since I get to do what I love doing best, which is play my flute. I mean, I suppose I could have gotten a summer job doing this in an orchestra. But have you ever hung out with people in an orchestra? I'm not talking about kids who are in orchestra at school. I'm talking about actual, paid classical musicians.

Yeah. Well, since I started going to Juilliard last year, I have.

And believe me, it is MUCH more fun to do what I'm doing, which is teach kids who've never seen a flute before how to play one. This rules. Because their eyes get so big when I rip through something really fast, like "Flight of the Bumblebee" or some Tchaikovsky, and then I tell them I can teach them how to do it, too, if they just practice.

And they're all, "No way, I could never do that." And I'm all, "No, seriously. You CAN." And then I show them.

That part kills me every time.

Skip says Ruth should have gotten an internship at some advertising company, and that these kids are never going to amount to anything no matter how much art we throw at them. He doesn't say that kind of thing to me, but that's only because he wants to get into my pants. The company he's interning for is paying his rent for the summer (which is why he is crashing on our couch: to save his rent stipend for something he really wants, which, knowing him, is probably something completely asinine, like a Porsche). He's here right now, as a matter of fact, sacked out on our couch (or, should I say, his *bed*), watching *Jeopardy!* with my brother Mike, who's also interning in New York for the summer, and also crashing at our place. (He gets the floor. Skip called dibs on the couch first.)

Mike—who ended up at Indiana University, as well, after having deferred admission to Harvard, due to being in love with a girl who later dumped him for a guy she met doing summer stock in the Michigan dunes. We are no longer allowed to mention the name Claire Lippman in our house—is in New York for a summer job that involves a think tank and computers and tracking cyber-terrorists. Sort of like what I was doing during the war, only he gets to do it from a cubicle on the Columbia campus instead of a tent in a sandy desert.

Sometimes Mike talks about his job to us. We all wish he wouldn't.

Both Skip and Mikey are yelling the questions to the *Jeopardy!* answers at the TV screen. Skip is getting most of them wrong. Mike is getting most of them right.

It's cool having one of my brothers around for the summer, even if it isn't my favorite brother. That'd be Douglas, and he's back in Indiana, renting a room from my parents.

But at least he doesn't LIVE with them, which is an improvement. He's renting a studio apartment above one of their restaurants, Mastriani's, which was rebuilt after a fire there. He works in a comic-book shop and has been doing some drawing of his own. I think he could have a career as a comic-book writer/illustrator. Seriously. I don't know if it's the voices he used to hear in his head, or what, but his stuff is really good.

So that's cool. Because for a long time, we thought Douglas wasn't going to make it at all, let alone on his own.

I personally never thought Skip would make it— without someone killing him for being such an annoying parasite—but according to him, when he graduates from the Kelly School of Business, which he is now attending, he will land a job making over a hundred thousand dollars a year.

So I guess I was wrong about Skip, too.

He's still annoying, though. Sometimes I let him

take me out anyway, because, whatever, free food. A girl could do worse. That's what my mom keeps saying. She would LOVE for me to hook up with old Skip, the hundred-thousand-dollar man.

Yeah. That's the other normal thing about me: I have no boyfriend. Not that Juilliard—not to mention the nonprofit summer job community—isn't rife with hot heterosexual guys. (I'm kidding. Because they totally aren't.) I guess I just haven't found Mr. Right. I thought I had, once, a long time ago.

But it turned out I was wrong.

So you can imagine my surprise when—just as Ruth was going, "Okay, seriously, you guys, we HAVE to get a share somewhere this summer. I mean it. Skip, are you listening? You're the one saving all the money, sleeping on our couch, you have to pony some up for the rest of us. I am not spending August sweltering in the Manhattan heat. I am talking Jersey Shore on weekends at least," and Skip and Mike were both yelling, "Orion! Orion!" at the television—there was a knock at the door and I went to answer it, thinking it was the pizza delivery guy, and instead found my ex-boyfriend standing there.

You would think a psychic would have a little warning about these things.

But then, that's what sucks about being me: I'm not a psychic anymore.

CHAPTER 2

"Jess," Rob said, looking past me into the living room, where Skip and Mike were sprawled across the couch like a couple of beached tunas. "Is this a bad time?"

Jess, is this a bad time?

That is what my ex-boyfriend says to me after what turned out to be two years or so of radio silence. Not so much as a phone call.

And okay, yeah, I'm the one who went to Afghanistan. I will admit that.

But need I remind you that it was TO HELP FIGHT A WAR?

It wasn't like I was out there HAVING FUN.

Not like HE was having, the entire time I was gone. Or so I can only assume, since when I got back, I found him in a liplock with some bleached blonde in a tube top outside of his uncle's garage.

Oh, sure. He said SHE'D kissed him. For fixing her

carburetor. He said if I had stuck around, instead of just taking off like a coward and running, I'd have seen him tell her off.

Yeah. I bet. Because guys just so hate it when blondes in platform heels with spray-on tans and boobs bigger than my head lean over and plant big wet ones on them.

Whatever. It wasn't like things had been going so great with him before I'd left for Washington and points east. My mom had not been, shall we say, thrilled by the fact that her then not-yet seventeen-year-old daughter was dating a guy who had not only already graduated from high school, but was

a) not going to college.
b) working as a mechanic in his uncle's garage.
c) from the "wrong side of the tracks," or, in the local vernacular, a "Grit."
d) on probation for a crime, the nature of which he would never reveal.

She didn't exactly make it easy on the two of us. The first (and only) night Rob came over for dinner, she pointed out to him how in the great state of Indiana, it is considered statutory rape if a person eighteen years of age or older engages in sexual intercourse with a person sixteen years of age or younger, a crime punishable by a fixed term of ten years with up to ten years added or four subtracted for aggravating and mitigating circumstances.

It didn't matter how many times I insisted that Rob and I were not engaging in sexual intercourse (much to my everlasting regret and sorrow). Mom just had to say the words "statutory rape" and Rob was gone, with a promise he'd be back when I turned eighteen.

I never even got to go to his uncle's wedding with him, the one he'd promised to take me to.

And then the war came.

And when I came back, having turned eighteen and lost the one ability I'd had that set me apart from all the other girls in town (besides my refusal to grow my hair out), I found him with Miss Thanks-for-Fixing-My-Carburetor-Here-Getta-Load-of-These-Head-Sized-Boobs.

He didn't see me. See him with her, I mean. He only found out I was back in town because Douglas told him when he stopped by the comic shop later that day, which, according to Douglas, Rob does periodically, to pick up the latest Spider-Man (which is funny, because I didn't even know Rob liked comic books) and shoot the breeze if Douglas is working the counter.

So Douglas told him I was home, and Rob came by my house that very afternoon, purring up on the self-same cherried-out Indian on which he'd given me that very first ride, so many years before.

He seemed pretty surprised when I told him to get the hell off my property. Even more surprised when I told him I'd seen him with the blonde.

At first I think he thought I was kidding. Then, when he saw I wasn't, he got mad. He said I didn't know what I was talking about. He also said the Jess he'd known wouldn't have run away just because she saw some girl kissing him. He said the Jess he'd known would have stuck around and knocked his (not to mention the girl's) block off.

He also said that I didn't know what it had been like for him, with me gone and him not knowing where I was, if I was getting blown up or what (because of course it wasn't like they'd let me call and tell people where I was, or anything like that, when I'd been overseas).

I guess it never occurred to Rob that it hadn't been any big picnic for me, either. You'd think he might have been able to tell, what with all of the newspapers trumpeting my ignominious return home, and return to normalcy ("Spark's Gone for Lightning Girl" and "Hero Comes Home, Psychic No Longer—Gave All to War Effort").

I guess it never occurred to Rob that I WASN'T the

Jess he'd known, the one who'd have knocked his block off. Not anymore.

I was the one who'd suggested a cooling-off period.

He was the one who said that maybe that would be a good idea.

And then I got the call from Juilliard: my spot on the wait list—I barely remembered auditioning. It had been during one of my leaves home—had come up. Classes started the very next day. Did I still want it?

Did I still *want* it? A chance to lose myself in music? The opportunity to get away from myself, the nightmares, the blonde with the head-sized boobs, my mother?

Did I ever.

So I left. Without saying good-bye.

And I never saw him again.

Until today.

Well, okay, that's not quite true. I guess I should confess that I couldn't resist forcing others (I would never do it myself, for fear that he might see me) to drive by the garage where he worked, so I, sunk low in the backseat, could try and catch a glimpse of him now and then. Like when I came home from school, at Christmas, and spring break, and stuff.

And he always looked as fine as he had that day I'd first met him, in detention, back at Ernie Pyle High—

so tall and cool and . . . just *good*. Know what I mean?

But he never called. Even when he had to know I was home, like over winter break. He certainly didn't drive by my house in the middle of the night to see if my light was on or to throw pebbles at my window to get me to come down.

I guessed he'd moved on. And I didn't blame him. I mean, I didn't exactly come back from my year away . . . well, whole. I certainly wasn't who I'd used to be, as he'd been only too quick to point out.

So I decided he wasn't who he'd used to be, either. Maybe, I decided, my mom was right. Rob and I were ultimately too different to be compatible. Our backgrounds were too disparate. What Rob wants—well, I don't know what it is that he wants, since I haven't seen him in so long. And now that I can't find people anymore, I don't know what I want, either.

But I do know Rob and I can't possibly want the same things. Because nowhere in my future do I envision a tube top.

It seems simplest just to tell myself that I want what Mom tells me I should want: a college degree, a decent career, and a nice steady guy like Skip, who'll make a hundred thousand dollars a year someday. Skip's a good sort of person, my mom says, for a classical musician to be married to. Because classical musicians don't make that much money, unless they're famous, like Yo-Yo Ma or whoever.

And the truth is, I'm too tired to try to figure out what I want. It's just easier to decide I want what my mom wants for me.

So that's why. About Rob, I mean. That's why I didn't fight for him, for what we'd once had. I didn't try to fix it. I was just too tired.

So I moved on.

Except that now here he was, a year later, standing in my doorway. He wasn't keeping his part of the (unspoken) bargain.

And he definitely looked whole to me. MORE than whole, in fact. He looked every bit as good as he had that day after detention, when he'd offered me that ride home. Same pale blue eyes, so light, they're almost gray. Same tousled dark hair, a little longer in back than my mom likes guys to wear their hair. Same jeans that fit like a glove, faded in all the right (or wrong, depending on how you want to look at it) places.

Seeing him, looking that good, standing outside my door, was a lot like getting . . . well, struck by lightning.

A sensation with which I am not unfamiliar, actually.

"Ask him if he can break a fifty," Skip yelled, thinking it was the pizza guy.

"Make sure he remembered the hot-pepper flakes,"

Ruth called from the kitchen, where she was taking down the plates. "They forgot last time."

I just stood there, staring at him. It had been so long since I'd stood this close to him. And everything was flooding back—the way he'd smelled (like whatever laundry detergent his mom uses, coupled with soap and, more faintly, the stuff mechanics use to get the grease out from beneath their fingernails); the way he used to kiss me . . . one or two light kisses, not even directly centered on my mouth all the time, then one long, hard one, dead in the middle, that made me feel as if I were exploding; the way his body had felt, pressed up against mine, so long and hard and warm. . . .

"This is a bad time," Rob said. "You've got company. I can come back later."

"Hey, can you break this?" Skip pushed past me, waving a fifty-dollar bill. He stopped when he saw Rob wasn't holding a pizza. "Hey, where's the 'za?" he wanted to know. Then he looked at Rob's face, and his eyes narrowed.

"Hey," Skip said in a different tone of voice. "I know you."

Ruth had poked her head out from the kitchen doorway. "Did you remember the hot-pepper—" Her voice trailed off as she, too, recognized Rob.

"Oh," she said in a very different voice. "It's . . . it's . . ."

"Rob," Rob said in that deep, no-nonsense voice that had always managed to send my pulse racing—same as, for some time now, the sound of a motorcycle engine had. It's like those dogs we learned about in Psych. The ones who would only get fed after a bell rang? Whenever they heard a bell ring after that, they'd start drooling. Whenever I hear a motorcycle engine—or Rob's voice— my heart speeds up. In a good way.

I know. Pathetic, right?

"Right," Ruth said, darting a worried look in my direction. "Rob. From back home." She refrained from calling him her private nickname for him: The Jerk. I thought this showed some real maturity and growth. Ruth's changed a lot since high school.

Well, I guess we all have.

"You remember Rob, Skip," Ruth said, elbowing her twin. "He went to Ernie Pyle."

"How could I forget?" Skip said tonelessly.

Okay, well, I guess all of us have changed since high school except for Skip.

"Right," Ruth said. "Well. Do you, um . . . do you want to come in, Rob?"

I didn't blame Ruth for sounding confused and not knowing exactly what to do. I didn't know what to do, either. I mean, a guy walks out of your life for a year,

only to reappear on your doorstep in another state . . .
It's kind of disorienting.

"What's the holdup?" Now Mike was crowding into
the tiny front hallway. He hadn't seen Rob yet. "You
guys need change or something?"

"It's not the pizza guy," Skip said over his shoulder.
"It's Rob Wilkins."

"Who?" Mike looked as shocked as I felt. *"Here?"*

"Look," Rob said, beginning to look a little impatient. I could tell from the way his dark eyebrows were
starting to constrict a little in the middle. It was the
same expression he used to wear whenever I'd want to
rescue some kidnapped kid using some wacky scheme
that Rob thought was too dangerous. "If this is a bad
time, Jess, I can come back—"

I could feel everyone's gaze on me—Ruth's, filled
with concern (she was the only one who could even
begin to suspect what kind of emotional whirlwind
Rob's sudden appearance had thrown me into); Skip's,
hostile and questioning (I had, after all, been dating him
pretty much exclusively all summer . . . if you can call
the occasional pizza and a movie "dating"); Mike's, also
hostile (he'd never liked Rob, primarily because he'd
never tried to get to know him) but also sympathetic . . .
Mike knew how hard I was running from my past.

And Rob was a part of that past.

Naturally, under so many people's scrutiny, I could feel my face heating up. Plus, I couldn't think of a single thing to say. Seriously. My mind was a complete blank. The only thing running through it were the words *Rob's here. Rob's here in New York.*

And he smells really, really good.

Seriously. It truly was like getting struck by lightning all over again. Minus the hair-sticking-up thing. And the star-shaped scar that had since completely faded away.

Ruth was the one who came to my rescue.

"We'll just go out and let you two have some time alone together," she said, starting to put the dinner plates down.

"Go out?" Skip echoed, sounding more indignant than ever. "What about the pizza we ordered?"

"You know what?" Rob turned to go. "I'll come back later."

It was only when I saw his broad, jean-jacketed back turning away from me that I realized I felt something. Which, for me, was progress. Since I hadn't been feeling too much of anything for a long time.

And what I felt was that this time, I wasn't letting him get away. Not that easily. Not without an explanation.

"Wait," I said.

Rob paused in the hallway and looked back at me. His expression was completely unreadable. And not just because the super still hadn't changed the burnt-out bulb above Apartment 5A.

Still, I could see his gray eyes glowing, like a cat's.

"Let me get my keys," I said. "We can talk while we grab something to eat somewhere."

I ducked back into the apartment, going to the skinny hall table where we throw our keys every time we come inside. Mike was blocking it.

"Move," I said.

"Jess," he said in a low voice. "Do you really think—"

"Move," I said, more loudly.

I don't want to give you the impression that I knew what I was doing. I most definitely did not. Maybe my brother sensed this and that was why he was acting like such a total tool.

Or maybe that's just how big brothers act when the guy who broke their little sister's heart shows up from out of nowhere.

"It's just," Mike said. "You really seem, um, better than you have in a while now, and I don't want—"

"Move," I interrupted, "or I will hurt you badly."

Mike moved. I scooped up my keys.

"I'll be back in a little while," I said, slipping out the door past Ruth, who gazed at me sympathetically through her new contact lenses. She'd given up wearing glasses at around the same time she'd given up on low-fat diets and gone high-protein instead.

"I thought we were having pizza," Skip called after me. I'd joined Rob in the hallway.

"Save me a slice," I said to Skip.

Then Rob and I headed for the stairs.

CHAPTER

3

New York isn't like Indiana.

Well, you probably know that.

But I mean, it's REALLY not like Indiana. In the town where I'm from, you don't walk anywhere. Well, unless you're my best friend, Ruth, and you want to lose weight. Then maybe you'll walk someplace.

In New York, you walk everywhere. Nobody has a car—or, if they do, they don't use it, except for trips out of the city. That's because traffic is unbelievable. Every street is clogged with taxis and delivery trucks and limos.

Plus, there's nowhere you'd want to go that the subway can't take you. And all that stuff about the subway being unsafe . . . it's not true. You just have to stay alert, and not look too much like a stupid tourist with your head buried in a map, or whatever.

But even if you are—a tourist, I mean—people will

stop and try to help you. It's not true what they say about New Yorkers being mean. They aren't. They're just busy and impatient.

But if you're genuinely lost, nine times out of ten a New Yorker will go out of his way to help you.

Especially if you're a girl. And you're polite.

Walking out onto Thirty-seventh Street with Rob, it hit me: you know, that we really weren't in Indiana anymore. I had never walked down a street with Rob before. Ridden down streets with him plenty of times. But strolled down a sunny, tree-lined street, with delis and pizza-by-the-slice places on either side, people out walking their dogs, bike-riding Chinese delivery-food guys trying to keep from hitting people?

Never.

He didn't say anything. He'd been silent down five flights of stairs (Ruth and I couldn't afford an apartment in a building with an elevator, let alone a doorman to announce our guests. And of course the intercom is broken, as is the lock on the door to the vestibule).

Now, in the busy after-work, trying-to-get-home-in-time-for-dinner crowd on the sidewalk, I realized someone had to say something. I mean, we couldn't just walk around in dead silence the whole night.

So I said, "There's a decent Mexican place around the corner."

But he just nodded. Sighing, I led the way. This was going to be even worse than I'd thought it would.

Inside the restaurant, I headed to my favorite table, the one Ruth and I share most Saturday nights, while I chow down on the free chips, and she plows through the guacamole (Ruth had finally managed to shed those extra forty pounds she'd been carrying around since sixth grade by avoiding anything with flour or sugar in it). The table is by the window, so you can watch all the weirdos who walked by. They don't call it Hell's Kitchen for nothing.

"Hey, Jess," said Ann, our favorite waitress, as Rob and I sat down. "The usual?"

"Yes, please," I said, and Ann looked questioningly down at Rob. I knew what Ann would say next time I saw her, and Rob wasn't around: "Who was the hottie?"

"Just a beer," Rob said, and after Ann had rattled off the restaurant's extensive list of brands, he picked one, and she went away to get the drinks. And the tortilla chips.

We sat for a minute in silence. It was still early for dinner—people in New York don't generally even start thinking about dinner until eight or even nine o'clock—so we were the only people there, besides the wait staff. I tried to concentrate on what was happening outside the window, as opposed to what was across the table from me. It was a little overwhelming to be in this place I'd been to so many times, with someone I'd never in a million years pictured being there with me.

Rob was nervous. I could tell by the way he kept rearranging the silverware in front of him. In a second, he would begin to shred his paper napkin. He was looking around, taking in the sombreros on the wall, the chili-pepper lights around the bar, and the people walking by outside. He was looking at everything, in fact, except me.

"So," I said. Because someone had to say something. "How's your mom?"

He seemed startled by the question.

"My mom? She's fine. Fine."

"Good," I said. I had always really liked Mrs. Wilkins. "My dad says she quit a while back."

Then I wanted to kick myself. Because, of course, the only way I could have known that Rob's mom had quit working in our family's restaurant was if I'd asked about her. And I didn't want Rob thinking I cared enough about him to ask my dad how Mrs. Wilkins was doing. Even though that's exactly what I'd done.

"Yeah," Rob said. "Well, what happened was, she moved to Florida."

I blinked at him. "She did? Florida?"

"Yeah," he said. "With, um, that guy. Her boyfriend.

Gary. Did you meet Gary?"

I had met Gary-No-Really-Just-Call-Me-Gary over Thanksgiving dinner at Rob's house. Apparently, Rob did not remember this.

But I did.

Just like I remembered what happened in the barn afterwards. I'd told Rob I loved him.

If memory served, he never did say he loved me back.

"Her sister lives there," Rob went on. "My aunt. And things were tight—you know, back home. Gary got a better job down there and asked her to come with him. So she said she'd try it out for a while. And she liked it so much, she ended up staying."

"Oh," I said, because I didn't know what else to say. Rob had lived with his mom in a pretty nice farm-house—old and small, but well-maintained—outside of town. They'd been pretty close, for a parent and kid. Rob had more or less been supporting her. I wondered if he resented Just-Call-Me-Gary for taking all that away.

"Well," I said. Because what else could I say? "I'm happy for her, I guess. For you both. That things are going so well."

"Thanks," Rob said.

Then Ann came over with our drinks and the chips

and guacamole. My "usual" is a frozen strawberry margarita . . . only without the alcohol, since I'm not twenty-one. I saw Rob look at it in surprise, and couldn't help grumbling, "It's virgin."

"Oh," he said. Then he blinked. "It has an umbrella in it."

"Yeah?" I shrugged. I took the tiny paper umbrella out, closed it, and tucked it into the pocket of my jeans. I am saving them. I don't know for what. "So what?"

"I just never would have pegged you for an umbrella-drink kind of girl," Rob said.

"Yeah," I said again. "Well, I'm full of surprises."

Rob didn't say anything more about my choice of drinks after that. There was a brief discussion over specials, but both Rob and I said we weren't ready to order yet, and Ann went away again, leaving us with the menus and our drinks.

I took a small sip of my margarita. I always take tiny sips, to make it last. The margaritas at Blue Moon—that's the name of the restaurant—are expensive. Even the virgin ones.

"And your folks?" Rob asked. "How are they doing?"

This was so surreal. I mean, that I was sitting there in the Blue Moon with Rob Wilkins, politely discussing our families. Like we were both grown-ups. It was sort of blowing my mind.

"They're fine," I said. I didn't say anything else. Like, "Oh, and by the way, my mom still hates your guts. And you know, I'm not so sure she has the wrong idea."

"Yeah," Rob said. "I see Doug from time to time."

Doug? My brother hated it when people called him Doug. What was going on here? Since when had Douglas started getting so pally with my ex?

"He told me Mike was spending the summer with you," Rob went on. "Ruth's brother, too, I see. Or is he just visiting?"

"No, he's with us until September," I said. "They're both crashing—he and Mike—while they work internships in the city. So did your mom sell the farm? I mean, when she moved to Florida?"

Which was my subtle way of asking what HIS living arrangements were. Because I was trying to figure out what he was DOING here. In New York, I mean. Suddenly, it had occurred to me that maybe he was here to, like, break some kind of news. Like that he was getting married or something.

I know it sounds stupid. I mean, for one thing, what would I care if he WAS getting married? I was just a girl who'd had a puppy-dog crush on him since the tenth grade. He didn't owe me any explanations, even if I HAD made the mistake once of telling him I loved him in a barn.

And why would he come all the way to New York just to tell his ex-girlfriend he was getting hitched? I mean, who even does something like that?

But these are the crazy things that go through your head when you're, you know. With your ex.

"No," he said, shaking his head. "We've still got the farm. Or, I should say, I've got it. I bought it—and the house—from my mom."

Which didn't prove anything either way. You know, about whether or not he was seeing anyone.

"And," I said, desperately trying to think of things to talk about, instead of the only thing I WANTED to talk about, which was what on earth he was doing here in New York. "Are you still working at your uncle's garage?"

"Yeah," Rob said, squeezing the slice of lime that had come with his beer in through the narrow opening of the bottle. "Only it's not his garage anymore. He retired. So he sold it."

"Oh," I said. Lots of things had changed in Rob's life since I'd been away, I could see. "Well, that must be weird. I mean, working for somebody else after working for your uncle for so long."

"Not really," Rob said, taking a swig from his beer. "Because he sold it to me."

I stared at him. "You bought your uncle's garage?"

He nodded.

"And your mom's house."

He nodded again.

With *what*? I wanted to ask. Because when I'd known him, Rob had never really been hurting for cash. But he hadn't been rich, either. At least, not rich enough to buy out someone else's pretty profitable business.

But I couldn't ask him that. What he'd used to buy out his uncle, I mean. Because we aren't exactly on those kinds of terms. Anymore.

"What about you?" Rob asked. "How are you liking school out here?"

"It's okay," I said. I wasn't about to tell him the truth, of course. That I hated Juilliard and had been miserable every freaking minute since I'd started there.

Besides, I was still thinking over what he'd said. He'd bought his uncle's garage. He was only in his early twenties, and he already owned his own business.

Just like my dad. I mean, my dad owns his own business. Several, actually.

And my mom *definitely* approves of my dad.

"Doug says you're doing really well." Rob started fiddling with his silverware again. "In school, I mean. First chair in orchestra, or something?"

"Yeah," I said. I didn't point out how many hours a day I had to practice to keep it. First chair in the flute section at Juilliard, I mean. "But I'm taking a break for the summer."

"Right," Rob said. "Doug says you and Ruth are doing some kind of summer arts program for needy kids?"

Douglas, I was realizing, had said a lot. I was going to have to call him when I got home and ask him just what in the Sam Hill he was doing, telling my ex so much about me.

"Yeah," I said. "It's pretty cool. I like it a lot. Better than playing in the orchestra, actually. The kids are fun."

"You always did like kids," Rob said, smiling for the first time since I'd opened the door and found him outside it. As always, the sight of that smile did something to my heart. Stopped it, more or less. "You were always great with them, too."

There was an awkward silence. I don't know what he was thinking during it. But I know I was thinking that things had been a lot better when I'd stuck to just that. Working with kids, I mean. It was when I agreed to start trying to find grown-ups that everything had gone to hell. Between Rob and me, I mean. And, actually, for me personally, as well.

"That's kind of why I'm here, actually," Rob said.

I glanced at him over the rim of my margarita glass.

"What? Because of . . . kids?"

"Yeah, basically," Rob said.

Without another word, I took a huge slurp of my drink. And got a brain freeze. And choked.

"Whoa," Rob said, looking concerned. "Slow down, slugger."

"Sorry," I said, wincing because of the brain freeze. I stuck the tip of my tongue to the roof of my mouth because that is what is supposed to cure ice-cream headaches, like the one I suddenly had.

But I didn't know of any cure for the heartache his words had induced.

Because it had all become clear. Why Rob was here, I mean.

He wasn't just getting married. He was having a kid. That had to be it.

And why not? He had his own place now, not to mention his own business. He was his own boss at last. The next natural step was marriage and a child.

Which was great. Really. Just great. I was really happy for him.

But why had he felt compelled to come all the way to New York to tell me? Couldn't he have just sent me a wedding invitation in the mail? That would have been a lot easier to handle than . . . this. I mean, did he have to come all the way here to rub my face in it?

"The thing is," Rob said, leaning forward a little in his chair. He had clearly seen that I'd recovered sufficiently from my frozen-drink headache. The heartache? That was still going on, but I guess I was doing a better job of hiding that than I had the brain freeze. "I know things have been . . . well, weird between us. You and me, I mean. The past two years or so."

Weird. That's what he called it.

Whatever. At least he realized how long it had been. Since things had ceased being hunky-dory (they had never been perfect) and started being . . . well, what he said. *Weird.*

"But we're still friends, right?" Rob's big shoulders were hunched as he leaned towards me. The ladylike little table at which we sat—the one decorated all over in mosaic tiles, which had always suited Ruth and me just fine—suddenly seemed too small, dwarfed as it was by Rob's man-sized body. "I mean . . . maybe we aren't—whatever we were—anymore."

Right. Whatever-we-were. That was the word for it, all right. Because what had we been, really? We hadn't really been lovers, because we'd never made love.

But I had loved him. A part of me still did. Maybe more than a part of me.

Because I'm a complete moron.

"But we'll always be friends, won't we?" Rob wanted

to know. "I mean, after everything we went through together."

I thought he meant the number of times we'd been unconscious in each other's presence, from being smacked over the head with various large, heavy objects.

But then he added, "Detention at Ernie Pyle High. That's gotta bind people for life, right?"

I smiled then. A tiny smile. But a smile just the same. Because it *was* kind of funny.

"Yeah," I said. "I guess so."

"Good," Rob said, leaning back maybe a fraction of an inch and his shoulders losing a pinch of tension. "Good. Okay. So, we're still friends."

"Still friends," I said. And took another fortifying sip of frozen margarita.

Because I really don't want to go to his wedding. Not even as friends.

"Then it'd be okay if I asked you," Rob said, starting to tense up again—I could tell by the way one of his denim-clad legs began to jiggle a little nervously beneath the tiny table—"I mean, as a friend—"

Oh my God. What if he's about to ask me to be his kid's godparent or something? I wondered who the kid's mother was. The blonde from the garage that day? God. I had so known he was lying when he'd said there was nothing between them.

"So," Rob said. "Here's the thing—"

I took a deep breath . . . and held it. Really, I'm a very strong person. I mean, I have lived through a lot in my nineteen years, including a schizophrenic brother, various fistfights brought on by people calling said brother cruel names, being struck by lightning, being stalked by the paparazzi because of a superpower caused by said lightning, sent to Afghanistan to help in the war on terror, and so on.

Heck, I've even endured two semesters of music theory at Juilliard, which, when I think about it, was almost as bad as the war had been.

But never in my life have I felt more need for courage I knew I didn't actually have than I did at that particular moment. I held my breath as Rob said the words I so didn't want to hear:

"Jess. I'm getting married."

Except that's not what came out of his mouth. What came out of his mouth instead were the words:

"Jess. I need you to find my sister."

CHAPTER

4

"**Y**ou need me to WHAT?"

He lowered his gaze. Apparently, it was too much for him to look me in the eye. Instead, he stared at his beer bottle.

"My sister," he repeated. "She's missing. I need you to help me find her. You know I wouldn't ask you, Jess, if I wasn't really worried about her. Doug's told me you don't . . . well . . . *do* that anymore. He told me the war—well, that it really messed you up. And I totally understand that, Jess. I do."

He looked up then and hit me with the full force of those baby blues.

"But if there's any way . . . *any* way at all. If you could just give me a *hint* about where she is . . . I'd really appreciate it. And I swear afterwards I'll go away and leave you alone."

I stared at him.

I should have known, of course. That it wasn't ME he wanted. Not, you know, that I'd ever once entertained the idea, since opening my door to find him standing there, that that's what he'd come for. To try to get back together, I mean.

And I will admit, it was a big relief that he wasn't here to tell me about his impending nuptials with Karen Sue Hankey, or whoever. Not that I cared what he did anymore, or who he married.

I just don't feel like I should have to know about it.

But to have come all this way to ask me to find someone—when he knew perfectly well how all of that finding people crap had messed me up—

Well, okay, he didn't know, really, since I'd barely spoken to him since it happened. The war, I mean. And the part I'd played in it.

Still, he had to have read it in the papers. He had some nerve coming here and asking me to—

Then suddenly something else hit me, and I looked at him confusedly.

"You don't *have* a sister," I pointed out.

"Yes," Rob said evenly. "Actually, I do."

"How could you have a sister," I demanded, sounding angrier than I'd meant to, "and not even tell me?"

"Because I didn't know about her myself," Rob said, "until a few months ago."

"What?" I couldn't believe this. I really couldn't. I mean, first my ex-boyfriend shows up at my door, and not even because he wants to get back together with me. Then he pulls out some kind of ghost sister. Seriously, this is the kind of thing that only happens to me. Wait'll the TV show's producers got a load of this. "Did your mom put her up for adoption, and not tell you, or something?"

"She's not related to my mom," Rob said.

"Then how can she be your sister?" What was he trying to pull? Did he think I'd lost my MIND during the war, and not just my psychic powers?

"She's my dad's kid," Rob said.

And then I remembered. You know, that Rob had a dad, too. I had never met him, because he'd left Rob's mother when Rob had been just a baby. Rob had always been reluctant to discuss his father—didn't even go by his father's last name, which was Snyder, but his mother's—until the day I'd accidentally stumbled across a photo of him, and dreamed about his whereabouts.

Which happened to be—for want of a better word—jail.

Rob had been even MORE reluctant to talk about his dad when he realized I knew where he was.

I just sat there staring at him. Because I seriously couldn't figure out what he was talking about.

"So . . . your dad's out of jail?"

It was Rob's turn to wince.

"No," he said. And I realized I'd never actually said it before. You know. The *J* word. It had always been an unspoken acknowledgment between us, back when we'd been—whatever-we-were. "No, he's still there. But before he got sent away, after he and my mom got divorced, he met someone else—"

Understanding finally dawned.

"So she's your half sister," I said.

"Right." Rob reached for a tortilla chip, scooped up a large amount of guacamole with it, put it in his mouth, and chewed. I doubted he was even tasting it. He was just eating it to be doing something with his hands, which always seemed to have needed to be doing something, since the day I'd first met him, either messing with an engine or folding over a paperback or kneading a rag. "I didn't know about her until she wrote to me this spring. See, she wasn't getting along with her mother, and so she started writing to my dad and he told her about . . . about me and my mom. So one night she called, and . . . well. It's something, to find out you have a little sister you never even knew you had."

"I can imagine," I said. Actually, I couldn't. I was just saying that to say something.

"Her name's Hannah," Rob said. "Hannah Snyder.

She's a great kid. Really funny and kind of . . . well, feisty. Like you, a lot, actually."

I smiled wanly. "Great," I said. Because, you know, that's the image I want the guy I'm in love with to have of me. Funny and feisty, like his little sister. Yeah. Thanks for that.

Not that I'm in love with Rob. Anymore, I mean.

"Things were . . . well, Hannah said things weren't great for her at home," Rob said. "I mean, with her mother. She was into some things—Hannah's mom—that she shouldn't have been into. Drugs and stuff. And men." Rob cleared his throat and concentrated on dipping another chip. "Men who Hannah said made her feel uncomfortable. You know, um. On account of her getting older, and them—"

"Paying unwanted attention to her?" I asked.

"Right," Rob said. "And I didn't think that was such a hot environment for her to be growing up in. So I started looking into what it would take for me to become her legal guardian until she turns eighteen. It wasn't as if her mother wanted her around. Since school was out, she—Hannah's mother—said it would be all right if Hannah came for a visit."

"Uh-huh," I said. But I wasn't really listening. A part of me was wondering how Rob could ever think he could get a court to give him guardianship of his little sister when he was on probation.

Then I realized he probably wasn't on probation any-more, for whatever it was he'd done. He'd been a juve-nile back when he'd done it, and now he was over twenty-one. That was probably part of some sealed court record somewhere, and now that he was a business and home owner—a contributing member of society—it couldn't come back to haunt him.

And I would probably never, ever know what it was he'd done that had got him put on probation in the first place.

"So a week ago, I picked her up from her mom's place in Indianapolis," Rob went on. "And Hannah came to stay with me. And everything was great. I mean, it was like we'd grown up together and never been apart, you know? We both like the same stuff—cars and bikes and *The Simpsons* and Spider-Man and Italian food and fireworks and . . . I mean, it was great. It was really great."

For the first time since we'd sat down, Rob's hands stilled. They lay flat on the table as he looked at me and said, "Then day before yesterday, I woke up, and she was gone. Just . . . gone. Her bed hadn't been slept in. All of her stuff is still in her room. Her mom hasn't heard from her. The cops can't find a trace of her. She's just. Gone."

"And you thought of me," I said.

"And I thought of you," Rob said.

"But I don't do that anymore," I said. "Find people, I mean."

"I know," Rob said. "At least, I know that's what you tell the press. But, Jess. I mean . . . you used to tell the press that before. To get them off your back. When they wouldn't let you alone, and it was upsetting Doug. And then again, later, when the government was after you to come work for them. You pretended then, too—"

"Yeah," I interrupted him. Maybe a little too loudly, since the couple who'd just walked in looked over at us, kind of funny, like *What's up with* them? I lowered my voice. "But this time it's not pretend. I *really* don't do that anymore. I *can't.*"

Rob regarded me unblinkingly from across the table.

"That's not what Doug said," he informed me.

"*Douglas?*" I couldn't believe this. "What does *Douglas* think he knows about it? You think my brother Douglas knows more than the thirty thousand shrinks the army sent me to, to try to get it back? You think Douglas is some kind of posttraumatic stress expert? Douglas works in a comic-book store, Rob. I love him, but he doesn't know anything about this."

"He might know more," Rob said, looking completely unaffected by my rather impassioned speech, "about you than the shrinks the army sent you to."

"Yeah," I snapped. "Well, you're wrong. I'm done, okay? And this time, it's for real. It's not just a put-on to get me out of the war. I'm out. I'm sorry about your sister. I wish there was something I could do. And I'm sorry if Douglas misled you. You shouldn't have come all this way. If you'd called instead, I could have just told you over the phone."

And spared myself having to see you again, just when I'd thought I'd finally gotten over you.

"But if I'd called instead I wouldn't have been able to give you this," Rob said, and reached into his back pocket and pulled out his wallet. I wasn't exactly surprised when he pulled out a photo—one of those school portraits taken on picture day—of a young girl who looked a lot like him. Except that she had braces and multicolored hair. I mean it. She'd dyed her hair, like, four different colors, blue, hot pink, purple, and a sort of Bart Simpson yellow.

"That's Hannah," Rob said as I took the picture from him. "She just turned fifteen."

I looked down at Hannah, the girl who was responsible for bringing Rob back to me.

But not, of course, because that's where he wanted to be. I knew the score. He was only back because of *her*.

And because, according to him, he and I are still *friends*.

"Rob," I said. I think at that moment I kind of hated him. "I told you. There's nothing I can do for her. For you. I'm sorry."

"Right." Rob nodded. "You said that. Look, Jess. I don't know what you went through during the—" He caught himself before he could say the *W* word and changed it to "—year before last. When you were . . . overseas. I can't even pretend to be able to imagine what it was like for you over there. From what Doug says, when you got back—"

I glanced up at him sharply. I was going to kill Douglas. I really was. What had gone on in our house after I'd gotten back—night terrors, the doctors had called them—was *my* business. No one else's. Douglas had no right to go around talking about them. Do I discuss Douglas's mental state with his exes? Well, no, because he has no exes. He's still going steady with a neighbor girl, Tasha Thompkins, whom he's been seeing for almost three years now, while she's taking classes at Indiana University and traveling back and forth every weekend to see him.

But if Douglas *had* had an ex, I wouldn't have discussed his private anguish with her. No way.

Rob must have noticed the angry flush I'm sure was suffusing my face, since he said in a gentle voice, covering my hand that held his sister's picture, "Hey. Don't blame Doug. I asked, okay? When you came back, you were so . . . you were—" He nodded at the small cactus sitting on the windowsill, amid more chili-pepper lights. "You were like that plant. Covered in prickles. You wouldn't let anybody get anywhere near you—"

"How would you know?" I demanded, angrily snatching my hand away and letting the picture drop to the middle of the table. "You were so busy with Miss-Thanks-for-Fixing-My-Carburetor, I'm surprised you even noticed."

"Hey," he said, looking wounded. "Take it easy. I told you—"

"Let's cut to the chase here, Rob," I said, my voice shaking. Because I was so angry, I told myself. That was the only reason. "You want me to find your sister. Fine. I can't find her. I can't find anyone. Now you know. It's not a lie. It's not a stunt to get people off my back. It's real. I'm not Lightning Girl anymore. But don't try to snow me with fake sympathy. It's not necessary, and it won't work."

Clearly stung, Rob blinked at me from across the table. "My sympathy," Rob said, "isn't fake, Jess. I don't know how you could say that to me, after everything we've been through toge—"

"Don't even start," I said, holding up a single hand, palm out, in the universal sign for Stop. Or Tell It to the Hand. "You only seem to remember everything we've been through when you want something from me. The rest of the time, you seem to forget it all conveniently enough."

Rob opened his mouth to say something—probably to deny it—but he didn't get the chance, since Ann came up to the table and asked, sounding concerned, "Everything all right here, guys?"

I noticed the only other couple in the place was glancing at us surreptitiously from behind their menus. I guess our conversation HAD gotten pretty heated.

"Everything's great," I said miserably. "Can we just get the check?"

"Sure," Ann said. "Be right back."

The minute she was gone, Rob leaned forward and, elbows on the table—his knees brushing mine beneath it and his fingers just inches from where mine lay by the picture of his sister—said in a low voice, "Jess, I understand that you went through hell the year before last. I understand that you were under unbelievable pressure and that you saw things no one your age—or any age— should have seen. I think it's incredible that you were able to come back and lead a life that bears any semblance to normalcy. I admire that you didn't crack up completely."

Here his voice dropped even lower.

"But there is one undeniable fact that you seem to be

overlooking about yourself, Jess, that apparently every-one but you can see: You came back from wherever you were broken."

I sucked in my breath, but he went right on talking, right over me.

"You heard me," he said. "And I'm not talking about the fact that you can't find people anymore. I'm talking about YOU. Whatever it is you saw out there—it broke you. Those people—the government—used you until they had everything they wanted from you—until you had nothing else to give—and then they cut you loose, with a thank-you and smile. And you came back. But let's not kid ourselves here: You came back broken. And you won't let anyone near enough to try to help you. I'm not talking about shrinks, either. I'm talking about the people who love you."

Again I tried to interrupt. Again, he stopped me.

"And you know what?" he said. "That's fine. You've rescued so many people, you think you're above letting anyone try to rescue *you*? That's fine, too. Rescue your-self, then . . . if you can. But let's get one thing straight: You may have been able to find missing people at one time. But you were never a mind reader. So don't pre-sume to tell me what I'm thinking and feeling, when you really have no earthly idea what's going on inside my head."

He leaned back as Ann approached with the check.

I stared down at the photo sitting between us on the tabletop, not really seeing it, I was so blinded by anger. That's what I told myself, anyway. That I was angry. How dare he? I mean, seriously, where did he get off? Broken? *Me?* I wasn't broken.

Messed up. Sure. I was messed up. Who wouldn't be after a year of basically no sleep, because every time I shut my eyes, I heard and saw things I really never wanted to hear or see again.

But not letting anyone try to help me? No. No, I had let people help me. The people who *really* cared about me, anyway. Wasn't that what I was doing, working with Ruth on her inner-city arts program? Wasn't that what letting Mike live with us was all about? Those things were helping me. I was beginning to sleep again. Most nights, all the way through.

No. No, I'm not broken. The part of me that used to be able to find people, maybe. But not ME.

Because if that were true—what he was saying— then the past twelve months of coldness between us— Rob and me, I mean—were . . . what? MY fault?

No. No, that wasn't possible.

Rob was fishing through his wallet for a couple of bills to pay the check. He wasn't looking at me. Instead, he stared out the window at a guy in a Sherlock Holmes outfit who was walking his pug. We see this guy a lot on our street. We call him the Sherlock Holmes Guy. Hey, it's New York City. It takes all kinds.

If Rob noticed the tweed hat with the ear-warmers and the curved wooden pipe, he didn't mention it. His strong jaw was set, as if to guard against saying anything more. He'd taken his jean jacket off, because the air-conditioning at Blue Moon wasn't the best. I couldn't help noticing the way the round curves of his biceps disappeared into the sleeves of his black tee.

No one at Juilliard has biceps like that. Not even the tuba players.

"I gotta go," I said in a strangled voice, and stood up so fast, I knocked my chair over.

Rob looked surprised. "You're going?" he asked. And his gaze fell to the picture in my hand.

Yeah. I'd picked it up. Don't ask me why.

"I've got stuff to do," I said, starting for the door. "I have to practice. If I want to be first chair in the fall, I mean."

Rob knit his brows. "But—" Then he glanced at my face. And stood up as well. "All right, Jess. Whatever you say. Just . . . look. I don't want there to be any hard feelings between us, okay? What I said—I didn't say it to hurt you."

I nodded. "No hard feelings," I said. "And . . . I'm

sorry I can't help you. About your sister, I mean. I'm sorry I can't . . ." Can't what? Be his girlfriend anymore? See, that's just it. He hadn't ASKED me to be his girlfriend.

He never had.

"I'm just sorry," I said.

Then I left the restaurant just as fast as I could.

CHAPTER
5

"Are you kidding me?" was what Ruth demanded, after I'd told her—in the privacy of our bedroom, since I didn't want Mike and Skip to overhear—what Rob had come to New York for. "Find his long-lost sister? He has some nerve, after the way he treated you."

"How did he treat me?" I asked. Because at this point, I was so confused, I didn't know what to think anymore.

"How did he treat you?" Ruth looked shocked. "Jess, he was making out with some other woman the last time you saw him."

"Not the last time I saw him," I said. "The last time I saw him, I was spying on him from the back of your car."

"I meant the time before that," Ruth said.

"The time before that, I told him we needed to take a break."

"And," Ruth said meaningfully.

"And," I echoed. "And what?"

"And he *let* you." She was perched on the end of her mattress, her blond curls framed by the purple sari she'd draped over the head of her bed, to give the room more "elegance." Though how you could hope to lend elegance to a room that was literally like, six feet by twelve feet, with a single window over which we'd had a metal gate installed so burglars couldn't get in, and more than its fair share of cockroach sightings, I don't know.

"He only did what I asked," I pointed out. "Look, he's not such a bad guy. I mean, I was head over heels in love with him in high school. He could have taken advantage of that. But he never did."

"Because he didn't want to go to jail," Ruth said.

I grimaced. "Thanks for that."

"Well, I'm sorry, Jess," she said. "What do you want me to say? He was a great guy? A perfect catch? He wasn't. And I don't care if he owns his own business now. He's still the guy who let you walk away when you needed him most."

"He says he tried," I said. "He says I was like a cactus when I got back, covered in prickles, and wouldn't let anyone near me. Plus, you know . . . there was Mom."

That's the nice thing about having a best friend. You don't have to elaborate. Ruth knew exactly what I meant.

"If he really cared about you," she said, "he wouldn't have minded the prickles. Or your mom."

I thought about that. The thing is, I wasn't sure. Both, I imagined, would have seemed plenty formidable—especially to a guy like Rob, who for so much of his life, didn't have much of anything . . . except his pride.

Which I'm pretty sure both my stubborn independence and my mom's disdain for him had injured . . . maybe even beyond repair.

Although . . .

"He says *I'm* the one who's broken," I murmured. "He says no one can fix me but myself, because I won't let anyone rescue me."

"Oh, so now he's a psychiatrist? What's *he* been doing for the past year?" Ruth asked with a sneer. "Watching *Oprah*?"

I sighed, then flopped back against my own mattress, which was covered with a nondescript brown bedspread from Third Street Bazaar. I had done nothing to lend more elegance to the room. The part of the wall above my bed was blank. I stared at the cracked, peeling ceiling.

"I just thought," I said to the cracks in the ceiling more than to Ruth, "that coming here would make me happy."

"Aren't you happy?" Ruth asked. "You seemed happy today, when you were showing that kid how to breathe from his diaphragm."

"Yeah," I said. "That part makes me happy. But school . . ." I let my voice trail off.

"No one likes school," Ruth said.

"You do."

"Yeah, but I'm a freak. Ask Mike. Well, okay, he's a freak, too." I restrained myself from pointing out that Ruth and Mike seemed to have a lot in common these days. I mean, they had both been übergeeks in high school who had "found" themselves—their true selves—in college.

And I would have to have been blind to miss the surreptitious looks I sometimes saw Mike shooting Ruth when she was in a cami and cutoffs, trying to beat the New York heat. Not to mention the looks she sometimes shot him when he came out of the bathroom with just a towel on, or whatever.

It was kind of revolting, actually. I mean, my brother and my best friend. Yuck.

But hey, if it made them happy . . .

"Skip," Ruth said brightly. "*He* hates school."

"Because school is just something he has to get through," I said, "until he can start pulling in that hundred grand a year."

"True," Ruth said with a sigh. "But I'm just saying. Most people don't like school, Jess. It's a necessary evil you have to live through, to get you where you want to be in life."

"But that's just it," I said. "I don't know where I want to be. And what little clue I do have . . . well, it doesn't involve playing in an orchestra, let's just say."

"But you like to teach," she said. "I know you do, Jess. And having a degree from Juilliard will look a lot better for that than having no degree at all."

"Yeah," I said.

I knew she was right. And the fact was, I was living many a musician's dream. I was in New York City, attending one of the finest music colleges in the world. I had instructors who were internationally famous for their skills. I spent all day immersed in the music I loved, doing what I loved doing best—playing my flute.

I *should* have been happy. I had seized the opportunity when it came along, because I knew it was the kind of opportunity that *should* have made me happy.

So why wasn't I?

There was a tap on the door, and Ruth said, "Come in."

Mike poked his head in.

"Is this a private party," he asked, "or can anybody join?"

Ruth glanced at me. I said, "Come in, stay out,

whatever. I don't care."

Mike came in. I saw him avert his gaze from Ruth's jewel-tone bra, which lay draped across the radiator. I saw her notice him notice it, and blush.

Oh, for God's sake, I wanted to groan. *Would you two just Do It already, and spare the rest of us?*

"So Skip and I were just talking," Mike said, and I noticed that Skip had crept in behind him.

"Yeah," Skip said. "And if you want us to, Jess, we'll beat him up for you."

I regarded the two of them from where I was sprawled across my bed.

"You two are volunteering to beat up Rob Wilkins?"

"Yeah," Skip said.

"Well, not beat him up, exactly," Mike said, darting a look at Skip. "But have a word with him. Tell him to leave you alone. If you want."

"That," I said, touched in spite of myself, "is so sweet, you guys."

"Are you insane?" Ruth asked both boys. "He could beat the crap out of both of you with one hand tied behind his back."

"Aw, come on," Skip said. "He's not *that* tough."

Ruth said, "Skip, we had to take you to Promptcare once because you got a quarter-inch splinter under your pinkie nail and you wouldn't stop crying."

"Come on," Skip said, looking embarrassed. "I was twelve."

"Yeah," Ruth said. "You know what guys like Rob Wilkins were doing when they were twelve? Smashing beer cans against their foreheads, that's what."

"Nobody needs to beat anybody up for me," I said to ward off a sibling-smackdown. "I'm fine. Really. Thanks for the concern."

"So what are you going to do?" Mike wanted to know.

"About what?" I asked. "Rob?"

He nodded.

I shrugged. "Nothing, I guess. I mean, there's nothing I *can* do. I can't find his sister for him, however much I might want to."

"How do you know?" Mike asked.

Both Ruth and I turned our heads to stare at him as if he'd lost his mind.

"I'm serious," he said in a voice that cracked. He cleared it. "I mean, you haven't tried to find anyone in, what, a year? How do you know you don't have it back? You've been sleeping through the night lately."

Everyone, including me, looked at the beat-up wood floor. The fact that I woke up everyone in the apartment with shrieks of unmitigated terror on a semi-regular basis was a fact that had always previously gone unmentioned by mutual agreement.

"Well," Mike said indignantly. "It's true. You seem to be doing better, since you started working with—"

"Don't say it," I interrupted quickly.

Mike looked confused. "Why not? It's true. Ever since you started—"

"You'll jinx it," I said, "if you say it out loud."

I didn't know whether or not this was true. But I wasn't taking the chance. I hadn't had a nightmare in quite a while. All summer, practically. And I wanted to keep it that way.

"But just because she's sleeping again doesn't mean she's got her you-know-what back," Skip said.

Ruth looked at him. "Skip," she said. "Shut up."

"You know what I mean," Skip said. "Her powers. You know. To find people."

"Skip," Ruth said again.

"And what if she does get it back?" Skip wanted to know. "That means they'll make her come work for them again, right? The government? Or the FBI, or whoever. Right? And then what's Ruth supposed to do? Find a new roommate?"

"SKIP!"

"I'm just saying, if she's got the ability back, why would she even bother with school and stuff when she could be raking in a fortune, hiring herself out as—"

"SHUT UP, SKIP!" Mike and Ruth both shouted together.

Skip shut up but looked defensive about it.

"Come on," Mike said to him. "*CSI* is on."

"I hate that show," Skip complained. "All we have to do is look out the window, and we can *live* that show."

"Then we'll watch something else, okay?" Mike shook his head as he steered Skip from our room. "Can't you tell they want to be alone?"

"Who? Ruth and Jess? What for?"

The door closed, as Mike tried to explain it to Skip. Ruth, meanwhile, looked at me.

"Are you sure you're okay?" she asked, sounding worried.

"I'm sure," I said, and picked up Hannah's picture again and gazed at it.

"I can't believe he had a sister all this time," Ruth said, "and didn't even know it. And he really wants to—what? Adopt her?"

"Be her legal guardian," I said. "I guess her mom's a crackhead, or something."

Ruth sighed. "Thank God you guys broke up. Right? Because it sounds to me like he might be in over his head. With a missing teen sister and all. Believe me, Jess, you would not want any part of that."

"I don't know," I said. "I guess not."

Ruth rolled her eyes. "Oh my God," she said. "Don't even tell me you'd help him. You know, if you still could. After the way he treated you."

"I wouldn't be helping him," I said. "I'd be helping her. Hannah."

"Right," Ruth said sarcastically. And got up to get ready for bed.

Right.

CHAPTER

6

At precisely eight o'clock the next morning, I banged on the door to room 1520 at the Hilton on West Fifty-third Street.

Rob came to the door looking bleary-eyed, wrapped in the comforter from his hotel bed, his dark hair sticking up in some very interesting tufts.

"Jess," he said dazedly, when he saw it was me. "What are you—how did you—?"

"Nice hair," I said.

He reached up and tried to mash down some of the tufts.

"Wait," he said. "How did you know where to find me?"

"I called your house," I said. "Why? Were you trying to keep a low profile? Because Chick was more than happy to tell me where you were staying."

"No," Rob said. "No, it's okay. I asked Chick to stay

there in case Hannah turned up while I was gone. I just . . . Sorry. I'm not really awake. Here. Come in."

I followed him into his room. It wasn't spacious—no hotel room in New York (that I'd ever seen, anyway) ever is. But it was nice. Rob was obviously making some decent change out of the garage these days, if he could afford digs like this.

"You want some breakfast?" he asked, still wandering around with the comforter trailing after him, like the train of a bride. "I can order us up some pancakes if you want. Oh, hey, there's a coffeemaker. Want some coffee?"

"Sure," I said. "But it would be simpler just to have it at the airport."

He threw me a startled glance from the little alcove where the coffeemaker sat. "Airport?" he echoed.

It was hard not to notice how adorable he looked, straight out of bed. Even with the hair. He kept the room very tidy, too, in spite of the fact that it was just a hotel room. His jean jacket was even hung up on one of those hangers you can't take off the pole.

"Airport," I repeated. "Do you want me to find your sister, or not?"

He said, still looking perplexed, "Well, yeah. But I thought—"

"Then I need to go back to Indiana with you," I said.

"But . . ." He'd loosened his hold on the comforter a little in his confusion, and I was awarded a glimpse of his naked chest. It was a relief to note that even though he was a responsible business owner now, he still had a six-pack. "But I thought you said . . . I mean, yesterday you told me—"

"I know what I said yesterday," I interrupted him.

"But—"

"Don't talk about it, okay?" I found that I was hugging myself, my arms crossed against my chest. I dropped my hands. "Let's just go."

He reached up to run a hand through his thick dark hair—which just made the tuft-problem worse. And also allowed the comforter to slip even more, so that I saw the waistband of his Calvins.

"Okay. But . . ." He stared at me. Having that blue-gray gaze on me, so searching, so penetrating, was almost more than I could take. I had to look at the floor instead of back at him. "You know where she is?"

"I seriously don't want to talk about it," I said. "Can we just go?"

But Rob couldn't let it rest at that.

"Honest to God, Jess," he said. "I didn't mean for— I mean, I just thought this whole thing with you saying you can't find people anymore was to get out of having to work for that Cyrus guy. Like it was last time. I didn't know it was real. I don't want you to do anything you aren't ready for. I don't want to . . . to disrupt this new life you've built for yourself."

Too late for that, isn't it? That's what I wanted to ask.

But what would have been the point? He obviously felt bad enough. No sense rubbing it in.

Which is not to say I wasn't glad he felt bad. He *should* feel bad, after what he'd put me through. I wasn't about to mention the fact that waking up an hour ago knowing where his sister was, after more than a year of not being able to find my shoes, let alone another human being, had thrilled me beyond words. I mean, that didn't have anything to do with HIM, really. It just meant that I was finally beginning to heal, after everything I'd been through. That was all.

And that maybe Mike was right. About the fact that since I'd started working with those kids of Ruth's, I'd started to dream again, instead of tossing around all night, lost in the throes of a never-ending nightmare.

"Look," I said to Rob in a hard voice. Because I wasn't about to let him know any of this. "Do you want your sister back or not?"

"I do," he said, nodding vigorously. "Of course."

"Then don't question," I said. "Just do."

"Sure," Rob said, reaching for the phone. "Sure, I'll call and book you a seat on the same return flight I've got. We'll go right after I've had a shower."

"Great," I said.

And watched as he dialed, asking myself (for the thousandth time that morning) what the hell I thought I was doing. Was this really something I wanted to get myself involved in? I mean, the progress I'd already made, just by being able to come up with an address for Hannah, was incredible. The shrinks back in Washington would have been throwing their hands into the air with joy if they knew, calling it a breakthrough. Why was I trying to push it, by going WITH him to find her? I mean, I could just give Rob the address and be done with it. Wash my hands of it. Go to work with Ruth, teach some more kids that there's more to life than video games and pizza by the slice.

But for an hour last night, before I'd been able to fall asleep, I'd lain there thinking over what he'd said. The part about me being broken, I mean. What if he was right? I was pretty sure he WAS right. Part of me *had* come back from overseas . . . different. Broken, I guess you could even call it.

And not just the part of me that knew how to find people in my sleep, either.

Maybe I HAD been a little hasty to condemn him for the Boobs-As-Big-As-My-Head girl. Clearly we had never worked as a couple, Rob and I. First the age difference, then the cultural difference, and then finally, the fact that I'm a huge biological freak had come between us.

But we could still be friends, like he'd said.

And friends help each other out. Right?

Rob didn't, I notice, ask me any questions on the way to the airport. He was following my advice to a T: doing, not questioning. Once we got through airport security, he bought me an egg-and-sausage biscuit—breakfast of champions—and an orange juice and himself some kind of waffle thing, which we ate in silence in the crowded, noisy food court at LaGuardia.

Maybe, I thought to myself, *he still isn't quite awake. Maybe he doesn't know what to make of my sudden change in attitude towards him and his problem.*

Which wasn't so odd, actually. I didn't quite know what to make of it myself.

Ruth had seemed to think she did, though. She'd rolled over at six, when our alarm went off, took one look at me, lying there staring at the ceiling, as I'd been doing since I'd wakened at five, and went, "Oh, crap. It's back, isn't it?"

I hadn't taken my eyes off the ceiling. There's a crack up there that looks a lot like a rabbit, just like in those books I'd loved when I was little about a badger named Frances.

"It's back," I'd said quietly, so as not to wake the boys.

"Well," Ruth said. "What are you going to do? Call Cyrus Krantz?"

"Um," I'd said. "Try *not*."

"Oh my God." Ruth rose up on one elbow. "You're going home with him, aren't you? Rob, I mean."

I tore my gaze from the ceiling and blinked at her. "How did you know?"

"Because I know you," she said. "And I know how you operate. You can never leave well enough alone. You can't just save the world. You have to micromanage every aspect of its rescue. That's why," she added wearily, swinging her legs from the bed and sitting up, "you'd make a crappy superhero. You'd stick around after the big save to make sure everybody's okay with what you just did, instead of just flying off into the sunset, the way you're supposed to."

It was good to know I had the support of my friends, I'd said sarcastically. To which Ruth had replied, with her usual early-morning cheerfulness, "Oh, shut up."

"Will you tell the kids I'll be back in a few days?" I asked her.

"You won't be back," Ruth said.

I'd stared at her. "What are you talking about? Of course I will. I'll be back in a couple of days."

"You won't come back," Ruth said again. "I'm not saying it's a bad thing. For you, it probably isn't. But just face it, Jess. You aren't coming back."

"What? You think I'm going to DIE tracking down Rob Wilkins's runaway little sister?"

"Not die, no," Ruth said. "But you just might let yourself get rescued after all."

"What's that supposed to mean?"

"You'll figure it out," she said darkly.

I didn't let her negativity towards the whole thing bother me. The truth is, Ruth's never been much of a morning person.

There are flights from New York City to Indianapolis every few hours from LaGuardia. Rob managed to get me onto the one he'd been planning on taking home. It wasn't a big jet, like the kind they used to shuttle people from New York to LA. After 9/11, the airlines downsized, and now when you fly to Indiana from New York, it's on one of those small planes you walk out onto the tarmac to get into. They only seat about thirty people, at most. And the quarters are cramped, to say the least. Rob had gotten us seats together—without, I'd like to point out, asking me if that was what I wanted. The flight wasn't full, and there were plenty of empty rows behind us where I could have gone and stretched out. Well, sort of.

But I told myself we were friends now, and friends stick together. Right?

It was a quick flight. I'd barely finished the in-flight magazine before we were landing. Rob just had a carry-on, same as me, so we didn't have to wait for our baggage to get unloaded. We walked straight out to where he was parked.

And I saw that he'd traveled to the airport on his Indian.

"Sorry," he said when he saw my face. "I didn't think you'd be coming back with me. We can rent a car, if you want."

"No," I said. It was stupid that the sight of that motorcycle should freak me out so much. "No, it's fine. Do you still have the spare helmet?"

He did, of course. The same one he used to loan me back when we—well, whatever we were doing back then. I put it on, then straddled the seat behind him, wrapping my arms around his waist and trying not to notice how good he smelled—like Hilton Hotel shower gel and whatever laundry detergent his mom—I mean, *he*—was using these days.

It was weird to be back in Indiana. The last time I'd been there had been over spring break. Buds that had only just been starting to show back then had now burst into midsummer bloom. Everything was lush and green.

Everywhere you looked, you saw green. There's green in New York—trees line almost every street. But the overall color is gray, the color of the sidewalks and streets and buildings.

Here all I could see was green, stretching until it met a cloudless, achingly blue sky.

I hadn't realized, until then, how much I'd missed it.

The sky, I mean. And all that green.

When we reached the outskirts of our town, an hour later, I saw that other things besides the buds had changed since I'd last been there. The Chocolate Moose was gone, sold out to Dairy Queen. Same building, new sign.

When we stopped at the red light in front of the courthouse, Rob turned his head to ask me, "Where to?"

"My house," I shouted back, over the thunder of his engine. "I need to drop my stuff off."

He nodded and roared off in the direction of Lumbley Lane.

And I soon saw that even the house I'd grown up in looked different, though the only thing that had changed was the color of the trim, which my mother had had spruced up to white from its former cream.

But the place seemed . . . smaller, in a way.

Rob turned into the driveway and cut the engine. I hopped off the back of the bike, then took off the helmet and handed it to him.

"I'll call you later," I said to him. "Will you be at home or the garage?"

He'd pulled off his own helmet. Now he looked at me oddly—as if he thought he'd done something wrong, but couldn't figure out what.

Welcome to my world.

"What about—" he started to ask.

"I said I'll call you." I didn't know how else to make him understand that I needed to be alone for this next part.

He looked a little angry as he jammed his helmet back on.

"Fine," he said. "Call me at home. That's where I'll be. I should check to see—I mean, maybe she came back by now."

"She didn't," I said.

He studied me through the clear plastic screen of his helmet. There was something he wanted to say. That was obvious.

But he seemed to think better of it and settled for saying instead, "Fine. See you later."

Then he turned around and drove away . . .

. . . Just as the screen door on the front porch of my house squeaked open, and my dad came out and went, "Jess? What are YOU doing here?"

I didn't tell them the truth. My family, I mean. That I was there for Rob, *or* that I had my power back . . . for now.

Sure, all they'd have to do was call Mikey. He'd have cracked under the pressure eventually—though I'd left him with firm instructions not to say a word to anyone about Rob's visit OR my apparently rejuvenated ability to dream.

But I knew it would be a while before Mike succumbed to the peer pressure to tell. Especially if he wanted to stay on Ruth's good side. Which I suspected he did.

Instead—after giving our German Shepherd, Chigger, the kisses he leaped up on me and demanded in his joy at seeing me home—I just told my mom and dad that I'd missed them, and had decided to drop in for a quick visit, using some of my airline bonus miles. It's amazing what parents will believe, if they want to believe it enough. Mine would never, I knew, shut up about it if they learned what I'd *really* come home for—to find someone. Worse, to find someone related to Rob Wilkins . . . whom my dad had actually always liked, up until I'd made the mistake of telling him about Miss-Boobs-As-Big-As-My-Head. Even then, he'd just gone, "But, Jess, are you sure about who was doing the kissing? I mean, if Rob says she was the one who started it, and he was just an innocent bystander, it's not fair of you to blame him for it."

Dads. Seriously. They should just stick to handing out the allowance.

My mom was delighted to see me, but mad I hadn't called first.

"I would've planned a barbecue," she said. "A welcome home barbecue, and invited the Abramowitzes and the Thompkinses and the Blumenthals and the—"

"Yeah, that's okay, Mom," I said. "I'm here for a couple of days. There's still time to plan something if you really want to."

"We could have a brunch," my mom said all gleefully. "On Saturday. People like brunch. And if they already have plans for the rest of the day, they can still do them, after brunch."

"Douglas is at work?" I asked, after dumping my stuff off in my room and noticing that they'd converted his room, across the hall, to an office for my dad, who'd formerly done the books from the restaurants at the dining room table.

"Probably," my mother said, as she fussed around, saying things like my sheets weren't freshened up, and how I should have called so she could run them through the wash first. "Or one of those city council meetings."

"What?" I grinned. "Douglas's interested in politics now?"

My mother rolled her eyes. "Apparently. Well, not politics, exactly. You know they're shutting down Pine Heights—" Pine Heights was the elementary school all of us had gone to. It was three blocks away—so close, we'd come home for lunch every day—a building constructed during the Depression by WPA workers, ancient enough that it still had two entrances, one for boys and one for girls.

At least according to the scrollwork over the doorways. No one, when I'd attended it, had ever paid any attention to the signs.

"There aren't enough children in the neighborhood anymore to fill it," my mother said. "So the school board's shutting it down. The city wants to convert it to luxury condos. But Douglas and Tasha"—Tasha was Douglas's girlfriend and the daughter of our neighbors across the street—"have some big idea about—well, he'll tell you about it when you see him, I'm sure. It's all he ever talks about anymore."

"Maybe I'll stop by the store and see him," I said. "If you think he's working now."

"He probably is," my mother said, rolling her eyes. "It's all he ever does. Besides this Pine Heights thing."

Which was funny, because just a few years ago, none of us would have believed that Douglas would ever do something as normal as hold down a job. It hadn't been that long ago, really, that we'd all despaired of Douglas ever even leaving his room, much less supporting himself.

"Invite him for dinner," my mother called as I banged out of the house. "Tasha, too, if she's around. I'll make your father grill some steaks."

"Hey," my dad yelled from his office-slash-Douglas's old room. "I heard that."

I left them squabbling and went down to the garage. Opening the barnlike doors—our house is a converted farmhouse, and almost a century old like most of the houses in our neighborhood—I went in and found what I'd been looking for: the baby-blue 1968 Harley my dad had bought me, as he'd promised he would, for high school graduation.

Not that I'd specified a year or color. Any bike would have suited me fine. The fact that he'd gotten me such a perfectly pimped ride had really been the icing on what was already some pretty delicious cake.

Still, with one thing or another—the war, and then my acceptance to Juilliard—I had only gotten to ride her a couple of times. I hadn't dared bring her to New York, where she'd have been stolen in—well, a New York minute. She was a real beauty, the color of the sky on an Easter Sunday—not quite turquoise, but not exactly teal, either. I loved her with an affection that probably wasn't normal. I mean, for an inanimate object.

But she was just so perfect, with her cream-colored leather seat and shiny chrome trim. My dad had gotten me a matching cream-colored helmet, which I put on after dragging her out from behind my mom's trim paint cans.

A second later, I was gunning the engine. It rumbled like the finely tuned instrument it was. Four months of disuse had done nothing to dull this beauty queen.

And then I was out on the street with her, feeling the tension that had settled in my neck—around about the time I'd opened my apartment door to find Rob there—finally starting to dissipate.

There is nothing like riding a really finely tuned motorcycle to get rid of stress.

But instead of turning towards downtown, where Douglas's comic-book store was, I turned Blue Beauty—yeah, okay, so I'd named my bike. I think we've already established that I'm a freak—towards the newer part of town, over by the big, multimillion dollar hospital they'd finished a few years ago. New apartment buildings had sprung up all around it to house the several thousand people who worked there.

Not the doctors, of course. They all lived in my neighborhood. The orderlies and nurses lived in this one.

Hannah Snyder, as I'd learned from my dream about her, was crashing in Apartment 2T at the Fountain Bleu complex just behind the Kroger Sav-On, right next to the hospital. I was surprised to see that there really was a fountain at the Fountain Bleu apartment complex. It was kind of a lame one, but it bubbled away in front of the complex in a somewhat soothing manner. All it needed, really, was a couple of swans, and it would be like the real Fountain Bleu it was named for, over in France. Or wherever.

I parked the bike and stored my helmet in its carryall. Then I strolled across the parking lot and thumped once on the door to 2T.

"Who is it?" a girl's voice asked.

"Me," I said. "Open up, Hannah."

She had no idea, of course, who I was. Not yet, anyway.

Still, I've found, over the years, if you answer *Me* whenever anybody wants to know who it is, they'll nearly always open the door, thinking *they*'re the dumb one for not recognizing your voice.

Rob's little sister stared at me a full five seconds before she realized I wasn't the "me" she'd been expecting.

But she definitely recognized me. Even though we'd never had the pleasure of making each other's acquaintance before. I guess she was up on her local history. Either that, or Rob had a picture of me somewhere.

Okay, probably she recognized me from TV.

She said a very bad word and, looking panicked, tried to slam the door in my face.

But it's hard to slam the door in someone's face when they're holding a motorcycle-booted foot against the door frame.

CHAPTER
7

"**B**etter let me in," I said.

Hannah made a face.

But she let go of the door.

"I can't believe this," she was grumbling as I pushed the door all the way open and invited myself into a stark white, fairly small living-room-dining-room-den combo. The paint still smelled fresh, and all of the furniture—a cheap leather set that reeked of no-payment-down—looked brand-new.

"He said you two were broken up." Hannah looked hot-cheeked and accusing.

"Yeah," I said. "We are."

I noticed a large-screen TV against the wall. She'd been watching Dr. Phil's most recent *Family in Crisis*. I wondered if she'd noticed any similarities between their lives and her own. I found the remote on the couch and flicked it off.

"Where is he?" I asked her.

"Who?"

Hannah had started to cry. Not because she was unhappy, I didn't think. I think because she was frustrated. And maybe a little scared. It's no joke when America's foremost psychic hunts you down. Especially when she's wearing motorcycle boots.

I guess Hannah doesn't read the papers much or she'd have known—you know. That I hadn't exactly been in top form lately.

I thought about telling her that she ought to be gratified that I'd found her at all. She was my first find in over a year. That had to be an honor, of some kind.

Except that to her, it probably wasn't.

"You know who I'm talking about," I said to her. "Where is he?"

"My brother?" Hannah sniffed. "How should I know? At the stupid garage, I suppose."

"Not your brother," I said. "Your boyfriend."

Hannah's mascara-rimmed eyes widened in an unconvincing attempt at looking innocent.

"What boyfriend?" she asked. "I don't have a—"

"Hannah," I said, "I didn't come a thousand miles to listen to lies. Somebody's paying the rent on this apartment. So tell me where he is, or I swear to God I'll have Child Protective Services here in five minutes flat."

I pulled my cell phone out of my pocket to illustrate the seriousness of my intent. Although truthfully, I didn't exactly have the number for Child Protective Services on my speed dial. I'd stolen that line from *Judging Amy*, one of Ruth's favorite TV shows, which she makes me watch in syndication at least five times a week. It is oddly addictive.

Hannah seemed to realize she was up against a force greater than her own, since she said with a defeated sniff, "He's at work. He's very important, you know."

"Yeah, I'll bet," I said sarcastically. "What does he do?"

"His dad owns this place," Hannah said with a flicker of In-Your-Face-Girlfriend 'tude. "The apartment complex, I mean. He helps run it."

Well, that explained the apartment, anyway.

But not the rest of it.

"So you picked a real winner, there," I said. Again with the sarcasm. "If he's such a catch, how come your mom didn't approve? And don't even try to tell me she did. Is it because he's too old for you?"

"She's such a bitch," Hannah said from the little ball she'd curled herself into on the leather couch. She was wearing jeans and a tie-dyed T-shirt. Between the shirt and her hair, which was still dyed to resemble spumoni ice cream, she was a veritable rainbow of color. "I mean, she brings home a different guy every week practically. But I tell her about Randy and she completely flips!"

I went to the window and pulled back the curtain liner. I could see the other side of the complex. There had to be over a hundred units altogether, making up Fountain Bleu Luxury Apartments. In the center of the complex was a pitifully small, kidney-shaped pool. A young mother sat beside it, as her kids paddled around in the shallow end.

"Where'd you meet him?" I asked, dropping the curtain and turning back towards Hannah. "Internet?"

She nodded. "A manga chatroom," she said. "Randy's a big manga fan. You know what manga is?" The look she darted me was sly.

"Japanese illustrated novels," I said. I wasn't about to mention that my brother had one of the foremost manga collections in southern Indiana. "Go on."

"Well, he asked me to meet him in a private chat room, so I did." Hannah was picking at the threads in a hole in the knee of her jeans. "And he was just . . . everything I've ever dreamed of. He asked me to spend the weekend with him, but when I asked my mom, she was like, no."

"So you told your newly discovered big brother, who is unfamiliar with the lengths teenage girls will go to get what they want, that your mom's boyfriends were putting the moves on you." I didn't need psychic powers to tell I'd hit the nail on the head. The truth was written all over her face. "And Rob believed you and invited you to stay with him on a trial basis. And you ditched him for this Randy guy the minute you got the chance."

She had the grace to look ashamed.

"I wanted to tell Rob where I was," she said. "Really, I did. But Randy said—"

"Oh, wait," I said, holding up a hand to stop her. "Let me guess what Randy said. Randy said your big brother wouldn't understand. Randy said your big brother would try to make something dirty out of it and maybe call the cops." Though most likely, Rob would have just beaten the guy to a bloody pulp. "Randy said that a love like the one you and he share is a sacred thing, not easily understood by us mere mortals. Did I leave anything out?"

Hannah blinked at me, looking hurt.

"You don't need to make fun of it," she said. "Just because things didn't work out between you and Rob, leaving you a bitter old maid, is no reason to assume every guy is a jerk."

"Oh," I said. "I see. Hannah, how old is Randy?"

"He said you'd ask that," Hannah said, getting up suddenly to go to the kitchen to get a glass of water. But I know she'd only gotten up so she wouldn't have to meet my gaze. "Well, not you, exactly, since I never thought—I mean, Rob said you were broken up. But Randy said people would try to make something dirty out of it, just because he happens to be a few years older than me—"

"How much older than you, Hannah?" I asked in an even voice.

"He's twenty-seven," she said, plunking down her water glass on the imitation granite counter. "But Randy says age doesn't mean anything! Randy says he and I knew each other in a previous life. He says we're destined to be together—"

"Hannah," I said in a hard voice. "You are fifteen. He is twelve years older than you are. His having a sexual relationship with you is actually illegal."

"Randy says the laws of man don't recognize a love that is as true as ours—"

"Hannah," I said. "If you tell me one more thing Randy says, I am going to smack you back into last week. Do you understand?"

She blinked at me, a little taken aback, but mostly still defiant. At least she was meeting my gaze now, though.

I leaned on one hip and said, "Look. You aren't stupid. You can't be, because you're related to Rob. So why are you acting like such a world-class sap?"

Her mouth fell open to reply, but I cut her off.

"You know all that stuff about the two of you meeting in another life is a load of bull. You know this Randy guy is after you for one thing. That's why your mom didn't approve, because she knew it, too. And you know the only reason you like Randy back is because he buys you things and pays attention to you and lets you live in this cool apartment where you can watch TV all day. Speaking of which, it's a beautiful day outside. Why aren't you at the pool?"

"Randy says—"

"Randy told you not to go to the pool, because someone might see you and start asking questions. Right? Doesn't that tell you something right there, Hannah? If this Randy guy really loved you, he'd have tried to get in good with your mom, not steal you from her. He'd have waited for you until you were legal, then asked you out, not hide you away in some apartment his dad's paying for. Sure, things are great right now. You can lounge around and do whatever you want. But what about when school starts in the fall? Are you just going to drop out? Be Randy's love slave for the rest of your life? That's a worthy aspiration for a girl of your intelligence."

She raised her chin at my sneering tone. She had spunk, anyway. I'd give her that.

"I hate high school," she said sullenly. "Everyone there is such a phony. Randy said he'd help me get my GED online—"

"Oh, right. And then what? Online college?"

"Randy says—"

"Oh, listen to yourself," I snapped. "Randy says this, Randy says that. Don't you have a mind of your own? Or do you just automatically do whatever Randy says?"

"Yes," Hannah said. She was crying openly now. And not from fear or frustration.

"Yes, you have a mind of your own? Or yes, you automatically do what Randy says?"

"I can see why my brother broke up with you," Hannah said with sudden venom. "You're really mean!"

"Oh," I said, smiling. "You think this is mean? I haven't even gotten STARTED yet. Get your stuff. Now. We're leaving."

She stared at me, dumbfounded. "What?"

"Get your stuff," I said. "I'm taking you back to your brother's house. And then I'm calling your mother, and we're all going to have a little talk about what is REALLY going on back at her house. And I'm betting she's going to say none of her exes ever hit on you. And guess what? I believe her."

Hannah looked about as shocked as a person who has grown totally used to getting her own way could look, upon suddenly finding things not going her way.

"I—I'm not going anywhere," she cried. "You try to drag me out of here and Randy—Randy will kill you!"

"Hannah," I said. "Let me tell you something. I just spent a year working with U.S. Marines, whose only job was to track down and detain men who'd trained at terrorist death camps. Compared to that, some twenty-seven-year-old pimp named Randy who doesn't even own his apartment is NOTHING to me. Do you understand? NOTHING."

Hannah's lower lip quivered. Her gaze darted around the apartment, as if she were looking for something to throw at me. I regarded her calmly, however, from the front doorway, which I was guarding in case the ever-fabulous Randy happened to come in unexpectedly.

"Randy's not a pimp" was all she could come up with.

"Not yet," I said. "Give him time. I'm sure, with the love of a girl like you behind him, he'll live up to his potential."

"I—I HATE you!" Hannah screamed at me. "You are such a BITCH! My brother is so WRONG about you! He goes on about you like you're some kind of PRINCESS. Did you know he keeps a SCRAPBOOK about you? Yeah, he does. Every time anything about you appears in the paper or some magazine, he clips it out and SAVES it. He's got like ten thousand pictures of you—God, he never even misses an episode of that STUPID TV show about you. He even made ME sit and watch it. All he ever talks about is how great and brave and smart and funny you are. I was *dying* to meet you someday, even though you totally ripped out his heart and stomped on it. And now I finally do meet you, and I find out you're nothing but a huge, giant, über-bitch!"

I could only blink at her, stunned not so much by her outburst—okay, not at ALL stunned by the out-burst—but by its content. Rob keeps *scrapbooks* about me? Rob watches the TV show about me? Rob thinks I'm brave and smart and funny? She thinks I broke ROB'S heart?

Boy, had she ever gotten THAT one wrong.

Could she possibly have been telling the truth? Could any of that stuff be even remotely—

"I HATE YOU!"

I ducked just as the lamp whizzed past my head.

Good thing, too, since the thing was made of brass, and ended up denting the cheap drywall, instead of my skull.

I straightened and glared at her with narrowed eyes.

"Okay," I said, "that's it. You don't get to pack your stuff. You're coming with me now, just as you are."

And I reached out and grabbed her by her ear.

Sure, it's an age-old technique, used by mothers worldwide to control fractious offspring.

But did you know the U.S. Marines use it occasionally as well, to quell a recalcitrant suspect? They do, actually.

Because it not only works, but it doesn't leave a mark. On the victim, I mean.

Oh, yeah. I learned a lot of useful stuff like that while I was overseas.

Hannah balked at first over being dragged by her ear from her boyfriend's cushy apartment to my motorcycle. But, as I explained to her, it was either that or I called the cops, and Randy got an extra-nice surprise when he got home from work that night, in the form of an arrest for statutory rape.

She finally gave in, but not exactly what you'd call graciously. I was strapping my helmet on her—I didn't have a spare, so I was going to have to risk my precious cranium to transport the little brat home—when she stiffened.

I knew without even glancing over my shoulder what she was looking at.

"Where is he?" I asked evenly. "And don't get any

ideas about calling him over here. I can dial nine-one-one faster than anybody you've ever seen."

"He's getting out of his car," Hannah said, her gaze devouring the object of her affections the way Ruth devours éclairs—or would if she went off her no-flour-or-sugar diet. "He's going to be really upset when he sees I'm gone."

"Yeah, well," I said, "I bet five dollars you never hear from him again."

"Are you kidding?" Hannah shook her head. "He'll go to the ends of the earth looking for me if he has to. He told me. We're soul mates."

Straddling the bike, I glanced in the direction she was staring, and saw a tall, skinny guy getting out of a Trans Am.

Seriously. Why do they always drive a Trans Am?

But instead of heading for Apartment 2T, old Randy headed straight for Apartment 1S. Hannah and I watched in silence as he thumped once on the door. It opened and a dark-haired girl, who looked even younger than Hannah, peered up at him. He leaned down and pressed a kiss on her that appeared to make her knees melt, since he had to drag her back into the apartment, as her legs apparently failed to work properly anymore.

Behind me, Hannah made a faint noise, like a kitten who has only just woken from a long, deep sleep.

"Huh," I said, gunning the engine. "Looks like Randy's got more than one soul mate, doesn't it?"

Then I got us out of there just as fast as I could. Without going over the speed limit, of course.

CHAPTER
8

Rob was on the phone when I tugged open the screen door and then pulled a very humbled Hannah into his living room.

His jaw dropped when he saw us. Then, remembering himself, he said into the phone, "Gwen? Yeah. She just walked in. I don't know. No, she looks fine. Yeah." He held the phone out towards Hannah. "Your mother wants to talk to you, Han."

Hannah's face crumpled. Then she turned and ran dramatically up the stairs, weeping the whole way. A second later, we heard a bedroom door slam.

Rob looked at me. I rolled my eyes. He said into the phone, "Gwen? Yeah. She's a little . . . upset. Let me go talk to her. Then I'll call you back. Yeah. Bye."

Then he hung up and stared at me some more.

"She's in love," I said, nodding my head in the direction Hannah's sobs were floating from.

"But she's all right?" he asked in a tight voice.

"Physically," I said. "I think a little visit to the ob-gyn might be in order."

His legs seemed to give out from beneath him. He sagged onto a chair at the dining room table.

"Thank you, Jess," he said faintly, speaking not to me, but to the carved wooden fruit bowl in the center of the table.

I shrugged. Gratitude makes me uneasy.

Particularly when it comes from someone who looks as fine as Rob does in a pair of jeans. It was so unfair that he should be so hot and at the same time so unattainable.

Unless any of that stuff Hannah had told me back at the apartment complex was true.

But how could it possibly—

To keep my mind from straying into this dangerous territory, I looked around Rob's place. It had been totally redone since I'd last been there. The chintz his mom had loved so much was long gone and replaced with masculine-looking—but still nice—olive-greens and browns. The flowered couch was nowhere to be seen, replaced by a brown suede one. The old nineteen-inch Sony was now a sleek plasma screen, mounted to the wall above a dark wood bookcase filled with CDs and DVDs.

Whatever else Rob might have been through since I last saw him, he wasn't hurting for cash. He'd converted his mother's place into a bona fide bachelor pad.

"You got any soda or something?" I asked. Because thinking about all the girls he might have been entertaining in said bachelor pad had left me feeling a little weak.

"In the fridge," he said. He still hadn't taken his eyes off the fruit bowl. There were three red apples and a banana ripening in it. If I wasn't mistaken, Rob Wilkins appeared to be in shock.

I went into the kitchen. It, too, had been totally remodeled, the old white farmhouse cupboards replaced by sleek unpainted cherry wood. The lucite counter was gone and a black granite one gleamed in its place. The appliances were all new, too, and were stainless steel instead of white.

I found two Cokes in the fridge and brought one out to him before taking a seat in a chair across the table from his. I figured, judging from the way he couldn't stop staring at that fruit bowl, his electrolytes had sunk as low as mine. Or something.

"Where'd you get the money for all this?" I asked, popping open my Coke can and nodding towards the plasma screen. My mom would have killed me if she'd heard me—it's totally impolite to ask someone how they got the money to pay for something. But I figured Rob wouldn't care.

He didn't.

"Dentists," he said. And looked away from the fruit bowl long enough to open his own soda can.

"Dentists?"

He took a long slug from the Coke, then sat the can down again on an expensive woven place mat.

"Sorry," he said. "Yeah, dentists. They're about the only people who can afford Harleys anymore. Well, and retired doctors. And lawyers."

I remembered the bike he'd been fixing up in his barn two Thanksgivings before. The bike he'd been fixing up when I'd told him I loved him. The time he hadn't said he loved me back.

"I get it," I said. "You've been buying old bikes, fixing them up, and selling them?"

"Right," he said. "The market for antique bikes is incredibly hot right now."

I thought about my bike, parked out in his gravel driveway. I wondered where my dad had gotten it. I can't believe I had never thought to ask. Had Rob—

But no. No, that would just be too weird.

"That's great," I said instead. "The place looks . . ." Move-in ready. God, what is WRONG with me? "The place looks really nice."

"Not nice enough, apparently," Rob said with a grimace and a glance up the stairs.

"Yeah," I said. "About that. She lied to you, you know."

"About what was going on with her mom?" Rob nodded. "I know. Now. Gwen—that's her mom—and I have been talking. Hannah snowed us both pretty good, it looks like. She told Gwen I was suicidal over a girl and that I'd begged her to come stay with me a few weeks to help give me a reason for living."

I thought back to what Hannah had said, about my breaking Rob's heart. So I guess it hadn't been true after all. It had all just been to get back at me.

But what about the scrapbook? And making her watch the TV show?

"She met him on the Internet," I said, and filled Rob in on the details about "Randy."

"I'll kill him," Rob said simply, when I was through.

"Well, you may have to stand in line," I said, and told him about the girl we'd seen in Apartment 1S. "I don't think Hannah's taking off is going to upset him for long. Looked to me like he had plenty of other sweet young things to choose from."

Rob gazed at me concernedly across the fruit bowl. "I don't want Hannah to have to deal with cops and testifying and things like that. I mean . . . she's only fifteen years old."

"I thought that's how you might feel about it," I said, absently picking up some papers that had been lying farther down the table, since it hurt to meet his gaze. "Hey. What's this?"

I held up the papers I had seized. They were a course catalog for Indiana University's College of Arts and Sciences, and a slip of paper with various numbers written on it.

"My fall class schedule," Rob said casually. "I've been taking night classes. You want another soda?"

"Sure," I said, looking at the courses he'd listed. Intro to Comparative Lit. Freshman Psych. Biology 101. "Geez, Rob," I said. "You own the garage, fix up old bikes, AND go to college part-time? And you thought you'd just add a teen kid sister to all of that?"

"I had it under control," Rob said in a voice that indicated his jaw was gritted. "At least—"

"Until the kid sister came along," I said. "Still. What were you thinking?"

"I didn't think she'd be . . . well, the way she is."

"What'd you THINK she'd be like?" I asked, taking the second can of soda from him.

"I thought she'd be more like you," he said, causing me nearly to choke to death on what I'd just swallowed.

"ME?" I gurgled. "Oh my God, you have to be kidding me. I was the biggest pain in the ass in the world when I was her age."

"That's not how I remember it," Rob said. But not in what I would call an affectionate manner.

"Yeah? Well, you can ask my parents," I said.

"You weren't like Hannah," Rob said, shaking his head. "I mean, yeah, you got in trouble. But it was for punching people, not shacking up with guys you met on the Internet. You would never have . . ."

His voice trailed off. The only sound in the house was that of Hannah's sobs, still coming loud and clear from what could only, I assumed, have been Rob's old bedroom. He'd have moved into the master bedroom his mom used to sleep in. I was pretty sure it probably wasn't pink anymore, either.

"Well," I said, because I couldn't, for the life of me, think of a solitary other thing to say. I mean, I wanted to ask him, of course. If what Hannah had said was true—about his having a scrapbook about me, and the part about me having broken his heart—

But Hannah had already told so many whoppers, it didn't seem likely that the ones I wanted most to be true were actually going to be the only truths she'd told.

Especially since Rob wasn't exactly giving off any Let's-go-back-to-whatever-we-were vibes.

On the other hand, he HAD just found out his kid sister had been seduced by a twenty-seven-year-old

Trans Am owner named Randy.

"I better go," I said. "I'm sure Mom's got dinner ready by now."

"Sure," Rob said. "I'll walk you out."

And the next thing I knew, we were strolling across his well-groomed lawn to my bike.

I wanted to ask him, then. You know, if it was one of his. But the truth was, a part of me already knew.

"She's a beauty," Rob said, nodding towards the bike.

"Blue Beauty," I said automatically, before realizing how cheesy it would sound out loud.

"She runs good?" he asked.

"Like a kitten," I said.

"I can't believe somebody ever gave you a license," he said with a chuckle.

"One of the few perks," I said, "of working for the government."

Then wished I hadn't. Because Rob's smile vanished.

"Right," he said. "Well. Thank you. I mean, for bringing her back."

I felt like a total and complete jackass. There was so much I wanted to say—so much I wanted to ask.

But all that came tumbling out of my mouth instead were the words, "I'm sorry."

He looked down at me in the purpling light, as the sun sunk down below the treetops, past the fields that surrounded the farm.

"Sorry?" he asked. "For what?"

"For," I said uncomfortably. *For everything,* I wanted to say. *For being such a freak. For listening to my mother. For ever letting you out of my sight.*

"For all that stuff I said to you last night" was what ended up coming out of my mouth. "For acting like such a total—um, überbitch, is how I believe your sister put it."

Something happened to his face, then. It seemed to twitch, almost as if I'd slapped it.

But instead of looking angry about it, an expression of—well, something I couldn't identify—spread across his face. And the next thing I knew, he had put his hand over mine, where it rested on the gearshift.

"Jess," he said.

Who knows what would have happened next if he hadn't been interrupted by a tinkling crash from the upstairs bedroom Hannah had locked herself inside? The crash was followed by an enraged scream. Hannah was having a tantrum.

The truth is, even if she hadn't . . . well. I doubt anything would have happened next, anyway.

"You better go deal with that," I said in a voice that didn't sound much like my own. That's on account of how dry my throat had grown, despite the two Cokes.

"Yeah," Rob said, dropping his hand from mine and glancing back towards the house. "I guess I better. Listen. Will you call me this time? Before you go back to New York?"

His eyes seemed to blaze in the twilight.

"So we can talk about what we're going to do about Randy, I mean," he added quickly, lest I make the mistake of thinking he actually, you know. Cared about me. As more than just a friend.

"Sure," I said. Even though I was totally lying. Because the truth was, I knew I could never be *just friends* with him. This was good-bye—whether he knew it or not. "See ya."

"See ya," he said. And turned and walked slowly back to the house.

I tugged on my helmet, relieved that, if he should happen to turn and look back—fat chance of that happening—the plastic shield would hide the tears that had sprung suddenly into my eyes.

God, I am such an idiot. First for falling for Hannah's lies, and then for ever believing—

But whatever. Really, what had changed? Nothing. He was still just a guy I'd—whatever-we-were—for a while.

Still. I mean, at least Hannah, messed up as she was, had taken a chance on the guy she loved. Sure, he was a jerk and obviously didn't care about her at all.

But at least she'd gotten some pleasure out of it. At least, I hoped so.

What had I gotten out of my relationship with Rob? Nothing but heartache.

The funniest thing? Those things Hannah had said Rob had told her about me—they weren't true. *I* wasn't the brave one. No, that was Hannah. Sure, I'd risked my life, plenty of times. But Hannah had risked something that, in the end, proved much more painful to lose:

Her heart.

I didn't look back as I drove away. Because I didn't want to see him close the door on me.

Again.

CHAPTER

9

I returned to my parents' house to find a party in full swing.

It's really something what my mom can do when she puts her mind to it. She'd decided she wanted to have a party to celebrate my (temporary) homecoming, and by the time I got back from rescuing Rob's little sister, a party was what was going on.

And okay, it was a bit on the small side for Mom.

But both Ruth and Skip's parents were there from next door, as was Douglas, with his girlfriend, Tasha. Even Tasha's parents, the Thompkinses, from across the street, were there, Dr. Thompkins out on the back deck with my dad and Mr. Abramowitz, swapping barbecue tips (not that my dad, a restaurateur and himself an amazing cook, was listening to any of theirs).

I had always felt uncomfortable around the Thompkinses, since their only son, Tasha's brother,

Nate, disappeared three years ago, and I had failed to find him . . . until it was too late.

But to their credit, none of them seemed to hold a grudge. This might be because in the end, I had brought their son's killers to justice.

Still, you would think seeing me would just bring back memories. A lot of people—including me—were kind of surprised the Thompkinses stayed on Lumbley Lane at all, considering the fact that the place could hardly have had good memories for them.

But they stayed. And came over to my parents' house for dinner quite often. Often enough, it would seem, for their daughter and my brother Douglas to have formed what was now the longest-lasting—and probably emotionally healthiest—romantic relationship of any of the three Mastriani kids so far.

"Hey, Jess," Douglas said when he saw me, and gave me what was, for him, a very uncharacteristic greeting in the form of a kiss on the cheek.

Sure, it was a shy one. But still. It was a far cry from how he'd barely been able to bring himself to touch another human being just three years ago.

"So Rob found you, huh?"

He asked this in such a quiet voice, at first I didn't hear him.

"Huh?" I blinked at him. "Oh, yeah. Yeah, he did."

"And did you help with that situation of his?"

"Yeah," I said. "The situation is . . . no longer a situation anymore. She's home safe."

"That must be a big relief to him," Douglas said, looking relieved himself. "He was really worried."

I studied my brother's lean face, with its fuzz of a beginning of a beard. And felt a spurt of irritation with him. "Thanks for the heads-up that he was coming, by the way," I said. "I mean, you could have called and warned me."

"So you could have run away to the Hamptons for the weekend?" Douglas grinned. "He asked me not to say anything."

And, apparently, Rob asking him not to say anything was more important to him than my emotional health.

"You and Rob certainly are chummy these days," I commented, not without some bitterness.

"He's a good guy" was all Douglas had to say in reply, before moving away from me to bring my mom a bottle of homemade vinaigrette from the fridge.

"Hi, Jessica," his girlfriend said, giving me a hug. I liked Tasha, not just because she'd followed my advice, and hadn't broken Douglas's heart. Which was a good thing, since I'd promised if she did, I'd break her face.

"How's New York?" Tasha wanted to know, in the wistful manner of someone who wanted to move to the Big Apple, but didn't feel like they had the guts.

"There," I said. I like New York. I really do. But. You know. It's just a town to me. A bigger town, maybe, than what I'm used to. But still just a town.

"And Juilliard?" Mrs. Abramowitz wanted to know. Mrs. Abramowitz always made a big deal about the fact that I was going to Juilliard . . . maybe on account of the fact that she'd secretly suspected I'd end up in a women's state penitentiary, and not one of the country's leading music colleges. She'd never come right out and said this, but I had my suspicions.

I started to give my standard reply—"It's fine"—but something stopped me. I don't know what it was. Maybe it was just being home.

But suddenly, I knew if I told her school was fine, I'd be lying. School wasn't fine. New York wasn't fine. I wasn't fine.

I definitely wasn't fine.

Only how could I tell her that? How could I tell her that Juilliard wasn't quite what I'd expected? That whatever free time I had, I had to spend in a practice cubicle, playing my guts out, just to keep up with the rest of the flutists at my level? That I hated it? That I wanted to drop it, but didn't know what I'd do instead? That New

York was great, it was thrilling living in the city that never sleeps, but that I missed the smell of freshly mown grass and the sound of crickets and the gentle weeping of Ruth's cello coming not from the other room, but from the house next door?

I couldn't. I couldn't tell her any of that.

"Fine" is what I said instead.

"And Ruth was good when you left her?" Mrs. Abramowitz wanted to know, as she helped herself to another margarita.

"Yes," I said, wondering how Mrs. Abramowitz would react if I told her of my suspicions . . . that there was something going on between her daughter and my middle brother.

She'd probably be delighted. Mike, like Skip, is well on his way to becoming a hundred-thousand-dollar-a-year man, only in computers, not business.

But whatever was going on between Mike and Ruth, it wasn't anything yet, and might never even come to be. So I didn't mention it.

"And Skip?" my mom asked in a teasing voice. Because, of course, my mom is head over heels for the original hundred-thousand-dollar man. Or at least the idea of his supporting me on that hundred thousand dollars.

"He snores," I said, and grabbed a bowl of dip to

take outside, where we were eating.

"It's his sinuses," I heard Mrs. Abramowitz tell my mom. "And his allergies. I wish he'd remember to take his Claritin—"

"There's my girl," my dad said with a big smile as I came outside with the dip. Chigger was suddenly all over me again, but this time it wasn't to say hello, but because I was holding something that contained food.

"Down," I said to Chigger, who obediently kept down, but who nevertheless followed me to the table with the assiduousness of a bodyguard.

"That dog," Dr. Thompkins said with a chuckle.

"That dog," my dad said, "knows over fifteen commands. Watch this. Chigger. Ball."

Chigger, instead of running to fetch his ball, as he normally did when he heard the word, stayed where he was, panting in the warm evening air, waiting for someone to spill some dip.

"Well," my dad said embarrassedly.

"He'd go get it, if there weren't food around."

I took a seat on the deck, lightly stroking Chigger's ears, and listened to my dad chat with his neighbors, looking out across the yard and the treetops beyond. It seemed weird that just that morning, I'd been looking through metal bars at fire escapes and into other people's apartment windows, and now I was gazing at a scene so pastoral and . . . well, DIFFERENT. I'm not saying one is better than the other. They're just . . . different.

I wondered what Rob and his sister were doing. I wondered what Randy and the girl I'd seen were doing. Well, scratch that. I had a pretty good idea what THEY were doing. I wondered instead what I should do about it. My options were somewhat limited, if Rob didn't want his sister to have to testify against the jerk.

But what about the dark-haired girl I'd seen? Surely she was underage, as well. If I went over there and happened to let the truth about old Randy having a little something on the side—right upstairs in 2T, as a matter of fact—would she come around?

But why should I? I didn't know the dark-haired girl. No one had asked me to find her. She wasn't my responsibility.

Maybe Ruth was right. Maybe I *would* make a rotten superhero. Because I really was incapable of just riding off into the sunset.

Mrs. Thompkins came outside, holding a salad, with Douglas following on her heels like Chigger had followed on mine.

"—should really come along," Douglas was saying as Tasha trailed after him, holding a platter of corn on the cob. "It's our community. We've got to take it back from the developers and yuppie corporate scum."

"But I just don't see the NEED for an elementary school in this neighborhood, Douglas," Mrs. Thompkins said a little helplessly. "The people who can afford to live here have kids in college, like we do, not kindergarten."

"That's why we're proposing a high school," Tasha said, her dark eyes alight with excitement. "Not an elementary school."

My mom had followed them out, holding her prizewinning scalloped potatoes in pot-warmered hands.

"Not this alternative high school thing again," she said wearily. "Can't we have one meal where we don't have to talk about this alternative high school idea of yours, Douglas?"

Which was pretty ironic, considering that just a few years ago, my mom would have given her right arm to have Douglas even SIT with us at the dinner table, rather than hide in his room.

"Fine," Douglas said, not taking offense. "But there's a community board meeting at eight. I'm hoping at least some of you can come."

"No politics at the table," my dad declared, brandishing a dozen perfectly charbroiled steaks. "Or religion, either. Both topics spoil the appetite."

Everyone ooohed and ahhhhed at the steaks, the way my dad had intended us to, then dug in. I ate with more gusto than usual, not having had much since my Egg 'n Sausage McMuffin that morning.

Sure enough, no sooner was dinner over than Douglas looked at his watch and announced it was time for the community board meeting, and that anyone who cared an iota for the neighborhood should stroll over to the Pine Heights auditorium with him and Tasha to hear what the board had to say about the future of the school.

None of the adults volunteered. Which was hardly surprising, considering the amount of beef and tequila they'd just consumed.

"Great," Douglas said sarcastically, when he saw this. "I thought you Woodstock generationers actually cared about the world."

"Hey," my mom said in a dangerous voice. "I was way too young for Woodstock."

"Jess?" Tasha had stood up to follow my brother out the door. "Want to come?"

I did not. What did I care what happened to my old elementary school?

"Jess doesn't even live here anymore," my mom said with a laugh. "She's a jaded New Yorker now."

Was that what I was? Was that why everything in my hometown looked so shabby and small to me now? Because I was a jaded New Yorker?

"Come on, Jess," Douglas said from the doorway. "Every locally owned business in this town is selling out to the chains. Look what happened to the Chocolate Moose."

"Not every locally owned business is selling out to the chains, Douglas," my dad pointed out dryly, meaning the restaurants we still owned.

"Do you really want to see the place where you played the mouse in *The Lion and the Mouse* in your third grade program turned into condos?" Douglas asked me, ignoring our father.

Well, it wasn't as if I'd had any better offers. No one else had asked me to do anything with them that evening. And if I stayed home, Mom would just put me on dish patrol.

I was touched Douglas even remembered that I'd played the mouse in my third grade program.

"I'll go," I said, and stood up to follow Douglas and his girlfriend.

They spent the three-block walk over to the elementary school filling me in on their proposal to turn Pine Heights into a high school—"An alternative high school," Douglas said. "Not like Ernie Pyle, which was so big and impersonal. That place . . . it was like an education factory," he added with a shudder.

Which was interesting, because I hadn't seen a whole

lot of educating going on there.

"The alternative high school would put an emphasis on kids working at their own pace," Tasha, who was an education major over at IU, said.

"Yeah," Douglas said. "And instead of the standard-ized state curriculum, we're going to have an emphasis on the arts—music, drawing, sculpture, drama, dance. And no sports."

"No sports," Tasha said firmly, and I remembered that her brother had been a football player . . . and how much attention he'd gotten because of it, whereas she, a shy and studious girl, had been almost the family after-thought.

"Wow," I said. "Great."

I meant it, too. I mean, if I had gone to a school like the one they were describing, instead of the one I'd gone to, maybe I wouldn't have turned out the way I had—broken. I definitely wouldn't have been struck by light-ning. That happened to me walking home from Ernie Pyle High. If I'd have been walking home from Pine Heights, which was so close to my house, I'd have made it home well before the rain started to fall.

It was weird being back inside my elementary school after all these years. Everything looked tiny. I mean, the drinking fountains, which I remembered as being so high off the ground, were practically knee-level.

It still smelled the same, though, of floor wax and that stuff they sprinkle over throw-up.

"Remember that time you banged Tom Boyes's head into that water fountain, Jess?" Douglas asked cheerfully, as we walked by an otherwise unremarkable drinking fountain. "For calling me—what was it? Oh, yeah. A spastic freak."

I didn't remember this. But I can't say I was surprised to hear it.

Tasha, on the other hand, seemed so.

"Why did he call you that?" she wanted to know. "Just because you were different?"

Different. That was one way to put it. Douglas always HAD been different. If you could call hearing voices inside of your head telling you to do weird stuff, like not eat the spaghetti in the school cafeteria because it was poisoned, different.

"Yeah," Douglas said. "But it was all right, because I had Jessica to protect me. Even though I was in fifth grade, and she was in first. God, Tom couldn't hold his head up all year after that. The snot beat out of him by a tiny first grade girl."

Tasha smiled at me admiringly, but I know there was nothing all that admirable about that situation. My high school counselor and I had worked long and hard to combat my seemingly uncontrollable temper, which was always getting me in hot water. I'd finally succeeded in getting control of it, but only after seeing for myself firsthand what could happen when someone with a bad temper got too much power—such as some of the men I'd helped catch in Afghanistan.

We walked into the school's combination auditorium, complete with stage, gym (basketball hoops), and cafeteria (long tables that folded up into the walls to get them out of the way during PE or Assembly). The room seemed ridiculously small compared to the way I remembered it. About ten rows of folding chairs had been set up before a long table, on top of which sat a scale model of Pine Heights school, only with the windows and landscaping redone, so it looked more like an upscale condo complex than a school.

Standing behind this model, glad-handing what had to be a bunch of city planners and local politicians, was a pot-bellied businessman in an expensive new suit . . . which couldn't have been all that comfortable in the summer heat, considering the school had no air-conditioning.

And standing next to the beer-bellied man was another guy in a suit, although this one was more appropriate for the weather, being silk. Also, the guy in it wore the jacket over a black T-shirt instead of a button-down and tie.

Except for the change of clothes, though, he was still perfectly recognizable as someone I had seen—albeit from a distance—just a few hours before.

Hannah's boyfriend, the two-timing Randy.

CHAPTER

10

"Everyone, if you could take your seats, please."

The city councilperson called everyone who was milling around, greeting one another—including my suddenly civic-minded brother—to order. We took our seats and sat there in the evening heat, some people fanning themselves with handouts Randy's dad had left on all our seats. The handouts described the complex he wanted to convert Pine Heights school into—a brand-new luxury condo "experience," with a gym and a coffee shop on the first floor. Apparently, more and more DINKs—double income, no kids—were moving to our town, commuting from it to Indianapolis. Such a condo "experience" would perfectly suit their needs.

People stood up and started talking, but the truth was, I didn't hear a word they said. I wasn't listening. Instead, I was staring at Randy Whitehead.

I guess I shouldn't have been surprised. I mean, we

live in a pretty small town. If a guy's dad owns one apartment complex, chances are he's going to own more than one. I mean, look at my dad. He owned not one, but three of the most popular restaurants in a town barely large enough to support a single McDonald's.

Still, it was a shock to see Randy, up close and personal. He seemed to be there strictly in a "supportive son" role, not saying much, and handing his dad things when it was Mr. Whitehead's turn to make his presentation. There was no denying that the guy was hot. Randy, I mean. If you like the hundred-dollar-haircut, loafers-without-socks type. Which I guess, to an inexperienced girl like Hannah, would seem pretty exotic.

To me, though, he looked like he would smell. Not of BO. But of too much cologne. I hate it when guys smell of anything but soap. Randy Whitehead looked as if he were DRIPPING in Calvin Klein For Men.

"The overall cost of each of these units," Mr. Whitehead was saying, "would be in keeping with the rising cost of real estate in a town that is fast becoming an extremely sought-after bedroom community for upwardly mobile workers in nearby Indianapolis. We're talking low to mid six figures, depending on the type of amenities buyers choose to incorporate into the overall design plan they select. In no way will the Pine Heights community suffer an influx of undesirably lower-income residents through this conversion."

Randy, while his father spoke, softly tapped a pencil. He didn't look like a man wondering where his soul mate had vanished to earlier in the day. He looked like a man who wanted to go home to watch some HBO and have a Heineken or two.

The community listened politely to Mr. Whitehead's spiel, asking one or two questions pertaining to parking and the school's baseball field, which was still utilized on a somewhat sporadic basis by families who enjoyed an impromptu game of softball on a summer evening. The baseball field would go, turned into a "lush green park area, open to the public, complete with a duck pond." This, in turn, led to questions about mosquitoes and West Nile virus.

What, I asked myself, was I still doing here? In Indiana, I mean. I had done what Rob had asked me to do. Why wasn't I on a plane back to New York by now? That's where my life was these days. Not here, listening to people freak out about a baseball field.

Of course, back in New York, I never really felt as if I belonged, either. I mean, everyone in New York was so excited about going to Broadway shows and having picnics in Central Park. Everyone but me.

Maybe the problem wasn't Indiana or New York. Maybe the problem was me. Maybe I wasn't capable of happiness anymore. Maybe Rob was right, and I was broken. Permanently broken, and would never find happiness again—

My musings on my seemingly permanent state of not caring about anything were interrupted by, of all people, my brother Douglas as he stood up and said, "I'd like to know how far the city council has gotten on its review of our proposal for Pine Heights to be turned into an alternative high school."

There was considerable murmuring about this. But not because people thought it was so out there or weird, as people have murmured over things my brother's said in the past. There was a general note of approval in this murmur. Someone at the far side of the gym shouted, "Yeah!" while someone on the other side said, "We don't want teenagers roaming around loose in our neighborhood."

"Alternative doesn't mean unsupervised," Douglas was quick to point out. "State certification will be required of teachers wishing to apply to work at Pine Heights Alternative High School. And like any school, loitering on school grounds after hours will not be permitted."

"But kids who go to so-called alternative schools," a woman I didn't recognize, but who evidently lived in our neighborhood, stood up to say, "are generally kids who've been expelled from mainstream schools. The troublemakers."

There was a murmur of assent from the crowd.

"Not our school," Tasha Thompkins stood up to say. "Our school will have strict admittance policies. Applicants will need to have references."

Back and forth it went between the supporters of an alternative high school and those who felt it would cause real estate values in the neighborhood to plummet. I sat there, not so much interested in the fight than in the fact that my brother—my brother Douglas—was leading it. My brother Douglas, who years previously had been interested in comic books and keeping to himself, in that order. Now he was leading—really, leading—a charge for change in a neighborhood he didn't even live in anymore.

And people were LISTENING to him. The boy who used to come home crying every day from school because some bigger kid had stolen his lunch money and called him a spaz. He was LEADING a group of citizens concerned about the direction their town was going.

And he was leading because he had a heretofore unknown—to me, anyway—talent for public speaking.

"The reason we're even here," he was saying, "is because the young people in our community can no longer afford to raise their children here. They're being priced out for homes in this community by people who don't even own businesses in this community, but choose to live here rather than in Indianapolis, the big city where they do business. Soon this town will become completely unaffordable to people my age. We're losing young people to big cities like New York and Chicago because there's no work for them here. Talented teachers are slipping away because there are no openings for them in our overcrowded public schools. Why not give us an opportunity to employ some of these people, pull them back into the local community, while at the same time, affording teens who might otherwise feel lost at the monstrosity that is our local public high school a chance to really shine?"

A few people clapped. Really, clapped, for something my brother Douglas said. It brought tears to my eyes. It really did. After the meeting ended—with an assurance by the city councilperson that both the proposed alternative high school and Mr. Whitehead's condo plan would be thoroughly reviewed and a decision made by the end of the month, I turned to Douglas and said, struggling to keep my emotions in check, "That was good, Dougie. Really good."

"Yeah," he said, still looking angry. "Well, not good enough. I think I swayed a couple of them, but that bastard Whitehead—he really has them snowed about the property values and turning this neighborhood into the Beverly Hills of Indiana. . . ."

"Don't worry," Tasha said, giving my brother a comforting rub on the back. "My dad knows the mayor. He promised to put a word in. I mean, after all, it's his neighborhood, too. And it's an election year."

"It would just be so cool," Douglas said, "if we could turn this place back into a school—the right kind of school, I mean. The kind of school you wouldn't have hated, Jess."

I laughed—not very easily—and then moved away as people came up to congratulate Douglas on his speech and strategize as to what the next step ought to be in their plan.

And I found myself standing not five feet away from Randy Whitehead, who was putting his dad's model into a big white box.

Before I even thought about what I was doing, I strolled over to him, leaned down, and said, "Nice model."

Randy glanced at me and gave me a big, capped-tooth smile.

"Thanks," he said. "You new around here? I've never seen you at one of these community board meetings before."

"You might say I'm new around here." I smiled back at him. "You?"

"Just moved here from Indy," he said. "Last year."

"That must be quite a change," I said. "Small town living, after life in the big city."

"It's surprisingly the same," he said. "I mean, mostly work, very little play."

I smiled even harder at him. "Come on," I said. "A guy as good-looking as you? You must get LOTS of play."

He ducked his head modestly, allowing some of his hundred-dollar haircut to fall over his eyes. "Well," he said. "Now and then, I suppose. How about you?"

I tried to look surprised. "Me? Oh, I don't have much time for playing."

"Really?" He'd successfully wrestled the model into the box. "Why not?"

"I'm too busy finding people, usually," I said.

"Finding people?" He regarded me with eyes that were the same color as Rob's. But somehow I suspected Randy's misty gray irises were the result of contacts. "What are you? A truant officer?"

"No," I said. "I'm Jess Mastriani. Maybe you haven't heard of me. I'm the girl who was struck by lightning a few years ago and developed the psychic power to find missing people."

He stared at me for a full beat. Then recognition dawned.

"No kidding?" He looked delighted. "Hey, I watch that show about you, sometimes. The one on cable."

"Huh," I said, in a small-world kind of way.

"Wow," Randy said. "It's really cool meeting you. I had no idea you were so young. In real life, I mean."

"Huh," I said again, this time in a gosh, really way.

"It is a real honor to meet you," Randy said, reaching out his right hand to shake mine. "I'm Randall Whitehead Junior."

"I know," I said, pumping his hand with vigor.

"You do?" He looked psyched to hear it. "Oh, right. Well, I mean, of course you do. You're psychic!"

"Not that kind of psychic," I said. "Actually, I know you through a friend of yours. Hannah Snyder."

Randy was a smooth one, all right. He didn't quit pumping my hand. But I felt it grow a little cooler in mine. And he blinked, twice, hard, at the name.

Then he said, "Snyder? I don't believe I know the name."

"Oh, sure, you do, Randy," I said in the same warm voice. "She's the underage runaway you were stashing in Apartment Two-T over at the Fountain Bleu apartment complex by the hospital. I found her there myself earlier today."

Randy dropped my hand. Like it was hot.

"I . . . I'm sorry," he stammered. "I don't know what you're talking about."

"Sure, you do, Randy," I said. And wondered what I was doing. My job was done. Why wasn't I riding off into the sunset?

But something in me just wouldn't let go. It was the only part of me, I suspected, that hadn't come back broken.

"Tell me something, Randy," I said. "Just between you and me. How many girls have you got living rent-free there, anyway? Two? Three? Or are there more? And how do you keep them all from finding out about each other?"

"I really—" Randy was shaking his head. "I honestly don't know what you're talking about."

"I'm afraid you do, Randy," I said. "See, I know all about—"

"Hannah Snyder is a very disturbed girl," Randy interrupted. "I'll just say she lied to me about her age, if you try going to the cops. And that she came on to me."

"Ignorance of the law is no excuse, Randy," I said. "If a person eighteen years of age or older engages in sexual intercourse with a person sixteen years of age or younger, it's a crime punishable in the state of Indiana by a fixed term of ten years with up to ten years added or four subtracted for aggravating and mitigating circumstances."

Randy blinked at me. "Th-there's no proof, though," he stammered. "Th-that it's me in the videos. You can't p-prove it's me."

Wait. What?

I smiled at him. "Oh," I said. "I think we can prove it's you, all right."

What was he *talking* about?

"I—I have to go now," Randy stammered. He'd gone as white as his dad's model of Pine Heights Condos. Then he practically fell over himself in his haste to get away from me.

A few minutes later, Douglas and Tasha found me sitting by myself on one of the folding chairs, trying to remember my lines from *The Lion and the Mouse* and failing.

"Ready to go?" Douglas asked me. "Tash and I usually go out for a cup of decaf after meetings. Want to tag along?"

"No," I said, standing up. "I thought I might go for a ride."

"Oh," Douglas said. But he was smiling. "Of course. You must really miss that, back in New York."

"You have no idea," I said. I wasn't talking about the bike.

"Well, thanks for coming along," Douglas said. "It was probably pretty boring for you, but, you know. I think it might have impressed a few people, seeing Lightning Girl sitting on our side."

"Yeah," Tasha said. "Randy Junior looked like he was about to barf after he got done talking to you."

"Well, you know," I said. "That's what I bring to the table."

"Shut up," Douglas said.

But he was laughing.

It felt good, I was discovering, to hear Douglas laugh. It was a sound I could get used to.

Not that I intended to, though. I had done, I felt, enough damage for one evening. I headed back to the house . . . and to my bike.

CHAPTER

11

I don't know what I was thinking. Maybe I just wasn't. Thinking, I mean.

My bike just seemed to sort of drive itself to the Fountain Bleu Apartments. There was no conscious decision on my part to go to that part of town. It was as if I looked up, and I was there, pulling back into the same parking lot I'd vacated several hours earlier.

Only this time, there was something there that hadn't been there before. And I don't just mean a lot more cars, since most of the residents of the complex appeared to have gotten home from work, and were currently enjoying their evening repast and/or a situation comedy on a major network (some of them, possibly, might even have been enjoying the show purportedly about me. If they had cable, that is).

No, I was talking about one car in particular. And that was a newish black pickup parked well to the back of the lot, where it wouldn't be noticeable, even though it happened to be in the exact spot I would have chosen, had I decided to perform any sort of recon on the place.

And since that's exactly how I'd decided to spend my evening, this put something of a dent in my plans.

Until I saw just who it was behind the pickup's steering wheel.

That's when I decided to tap on the driver's-side window, having stashed my bike in the lot next door in an effort to remain unobtrusive.

Rob, startled, rolled down his window.

"What are you doing here?" he asked in some surprise.

But he couldn't have been as surprised as I was. Because I could hear what he was listening to inside the pickup's cab.

And it was Tchaikovsky.

"I thought I'd pay a call on the young lady living in One-S," I said. Why was he listening to classical music? Did he even *like* classical music? I guess so. All this time, and I never even knew that about him. What else didn't I know about him? "How about you?"

"I'm waiting for young Master Whitehead to get home," Rob replied pleasantly. "After which point, I'm going to beat him senseless."

"Hannah told you his full name?" I was surprised. I

hadn't thought she'd be so forthcoming with her half brother, who she must have suspected did not have Randy's best intentions at heart.

"No," he said. "I Googled who owns the Fountain Bleu apartment complex, and found a pic of Randy Junior. I was going to kick his ass tomorrow, after Hannah's mom got here to pick her up. But Chick volunteered to keep an eye on her while I was gone, so I was able to change my plans."

"You're not going to let Hannah stay?" I asked.

Rob made an incredulous noise. "Are you kidding me? I'm clearly the last guy who should be raising a teenage girl. She tricked me as easily—well, as you used to trick your parents."

I chose to ignore that.

"So what's the plan?" I asked him. "You're just going to wait until he pulls up, then have a blanket party?" I was referring to the age-old Hoosier tradition of throwing a blanket over a victim's head, then beating him with a baseball bat, or bars of soap slipped into the end of a sock.

"No," Rob said mildly. "I'm skipping the blanket. I was thinking I'd like to see his face as I grind it into the pavement."

"Right," I said. "Well, good luck with that. I just saw him at a city council meeting, where I told him I was onto him, so he's probably either already been here to pick up his other girlfriend and left, or is going to stay far away from this place for the time being."

Rob looked crushed. "Are you kidding me?"

"I'm not," I said. "Sorry. But you can still make yourself useful."

He lifted a quizzical brow. "Really. How?"

"Honk if the cops show up," I said with a wink.

Then I turned to head towards the apartment complex.

As I'd expected, behind me, a car door opened, then slammed shut. A second later, Rob's voice sounded just behind me.

"Mastriani," he said, sounding suspicious. "What are you doing?"

"Oh," I said with a shrug. "Randy mentioned something that made me want to come over here and check the place out. That's all."

"What do you mean, check the place out?" Rob demanded. It was quiet in the Fountain Bleu apartment complex. Except for the burbling of the fountain and the trill of crickets, that is. Even the swimming pool was empty. The only other sounds were our footsteps, as we headed towards Apartment 1S.

"Just something Randy said," I told him. "It could be nothing. Or it could be something. But I'm pretty sure you're not really going to want to be a party to what I'm about to do, since it will probably involve some breaking and entering. And with your police record . . ."

"I don't have a police record," Rob said. "I have a juvenile record. And it's sealed."

I don't know why he added this last part. What did he think I was going to do, log on to some kind of government computer and try to look up his file to see what it was he'd done so long ago that had gotten him into so much hot water? Because of course I'd already tried that, and gotten nothing.

"Fine," I said. "Then you can be the lookout."

"Lookout nothing," Rob said. "I'm in this, Mastriani. You're not shutting me out. Not this time."

I stole a glance up at his face. His jaw was set, his brow lowered with irritation. Me, shut *him* out? Wasn't it the other way around?

But I didn't ask the question out loud. Instead I said, "Fine. But if you're going to tag along, you have to do things my way. And my way doesn't involve anyone getting beaten senseless."

Rob actually looked surprised. "Now you really *are* kidding," he said.

"Actually, I'm not. I don't do violence anymore." I was careful not to look at him as we headed towards the door marked 1S. "I've learned there are more effective

· 137 ·

ways of solving problems than ramming your fist into your adversary's face."

"I'm impressed." A glance at his face showed me that he wasn't being sarcastic. He was smiling a little. "Mr. Goodhart would be proud."

I thought about my high school guidance counselor, and his efforts to curb my quick temper—and fists. None of his suggestions had been as effective as seeing for myself, firsthand, the kind of devastation a too-hasty decision to act first and ask questions later could cause.

"Yes," I said, thinking fondly of Mr. Goodhart. "He would, actually."

Then I reached up and thumped on the door to the apartment Randy apparently shared with the dark-haired girl I'd seen him kissing earlier. When, to my surprise, no one answered, I tried the knob. Hey, you never know.

But it was locked.

"This where you found Hannah?" Rob wanted to know.

"No," I said. "Hannah was in Two-T."

"Oh. So, what now?" Rob wanted to know, even as I was digging in my back pocket for my wallet.

"Now it's time for a little B and E," I said. "Try to look casual. Hey, you got a credit card on you?"

"That you can destroy trying to open that door? No."

"Never mind," I said, finding a card I could use in my wallet. "I'm good." And I slipped the card between the doorjamb and the knob. It was a trick that would never have worked on our apartment in New York, where we had a dead bolt.

But who needs a dead bolt in a sleepy town like this one?

Unless, of course, you're Randy Whitehead, and you're up to the kind of things I suspected Randy was up to.

"Hey," Rob said softly, when he saw the card I was using to push the lock back. "Aren't you going to need that in the fall?"

I looked down at the photo of my own face, staring back up at me from the front of my Juilliard ID card. You'd have thought, seeing as how the day I'd had that picture taken, I was starting a whole new life, at a school I'd always wanted to go to, where I'd be doing what I loved best to do in the world all day long, that I'd have looked excited and happy in my photo.

Instead I looked cranky and sort of annoyed. I had gotten lost on the subway on the way to my appointment, and I had been hot and exhausted, and a homeless guy had just spat on me for no reason.

Oh, yeah. I love New York, all right.

"I can always get a new one," I said with a shrug, not

mentioning the forty-dollar lost ID replacement fee. Or the fact that the thought of going back to school in the fall made me feel like I might barf.

And then, just as my photo got nearly all the way peeled off the card, the door opened a fraction of an inch.

I put my finger to my lips and looked meaningfully at Rob. Then I pushed the door the rest of the way open and called into the apartment, "Randy? You around?"

But I could see by the fact that none of the lights was on that no one was there.

I reached around the doorjamb and flicked on the overheads. They shined down on an apartment that was almost exactly like the one upstairs in which I'd found Hannah, even down to the same hideous leather living room set.

I signaled for Rob to follow me into the apartment, then shut the door behind us.

"So," he said, looking around the nondescript—and, frankly, depressing—living room. "What now? We going to wait and jump him when he gets home?"

"No," I said. "I told you. I don't do that kind of thing anymore. And if you're going to hang around with me, you can't, either. There are better ways to make someone sorry for what they've done than smacking them."

"Really?" Rob had stooped to pick up a magazine someone had left lying on the glass-topped coffee table in front of the flat-screen television. *Teen People*. "I'd be interested in hearing about them."

"Watch and learn, my friend," I said, heading to the bedroom. "Watch and learn."

The bedroom was as depressing as the living room. Not because it was drab or poorly furnished. The opposite, in fact. The king-size bed was covered in a tasteful beige spread, the walls decorated with nicely framed Monet prints. There was an expensive gilt mirror above the long, modern-looking dresser, and the bathroom fixtures were top of the line.

It was a room that simply bore no hint of the personality of the person who lived in it. There was a hairbrush on the vanity, and a scattering of makeup. In the closet hung a few dresses and tops of a style that indicated their owner was young and reasonably attractive—or at least assured of her own good looks, since they were pretty skimpy.

But there were no photos, no books, no CDs—nothing at all, really, that gave any hint as to who the dark-haired girl really was.

"What are we looking for?" Rob wanted to know, pulling open dresser drawers and finding only jeans and—somewhat provocative—underwear in them.

"I'll tell you when I see it," I said, looking around the room. There was a smoke detector on the ceiling, centered directly over the bed.

"Maybe he went to his parents' house," Rob said, meaning Randy. "They live right here in town, you know. Over in that new subdivision behind the mall."

"What new subdivision behind the mall?" I asked, startled.

"The one Randy Whitehead Senior built," Rob said, looking surprised I didn't know about it. Then he said, "Oh, that's right. It was while you were gone. Well, he built a new subdivision. It's full of five-, six-bedroom homes with three-car garages and in-ground pools."

"McMansions," I said.

"Right. I bet that's where we'll find Randy," Rob said. "Holed up with Mom and Dad. They probably have a security system, even the subdivision is gated."

I raised my eyebrows. "A gated community? Here in town? Seriously?"

"Keep out the riffraff," Rob said. "And enraged older brothers who want to beat Randy's face in."

"We're not looking for Randy," I said, staring at my reflection in the gilt mirror above the dresser. The king-size bed was directly behind me.

"Well, what *are* we looking for?" Rob wanted to know.

"I told you," I said. "I'll let you know when I find it. Help me move this mirror."

Rob looked at the mirror, which was huge. "No way. It's probably bolted to the wall."

"It isn't," I said simply, and moved to put my hands under one end of the frame. "Come on. Lift."

Rob went to the other end of the mirror, and together we lifted it off the wall. It wasn't easy—the thing weighed a ton. And with the dresser in the way, it was hard to balance.

But eventually we got the mirror down, and leaned it up against the bed.

Then we both stared at the spot in the middle of the wall where the mirror had hung. The spot where a section of the wall had been cut out and a video camera tucked inside, where it had apparently been filming through the glass in the mirror, which was apparently not a mirror at all, but a piece of two-way.

Rob, seeing the camera, said a very bad word.

"Remember how you told me to tell you what we were looking for?" I said. "And I said I would when we found it? Well, we found it."

CHAPTER

12

"**B**ut, seriously, Jess," Rob said. "How'd you know?"

"I didn't," I said. We were sitting on the floor of the walk-in bedroom closet of Apartment 1S. Around us lay a pile of men's shoes. They were what we'd pulled down from the closet shelf on which the video camera sat, pointing through the hole in the closet wall into the bedroom. Randy had obviously hidden the camera from view under piles of Adidas and JP Tod's driving moccasins.

"I just guessed," I said. "Something he said."

Rob looked at the tapes we'd pulled down from a closet shelf high above our heads—I'd had to be lifted to reach it. Randy obviously used a stepladder. Each tape was neatly labeled with a name. CARLY. JASMINE. ALLISON. RACHEL. BETH.

There were multiple copies of each. Sadly, I think we were going to have to watch them in order to see if they were multiple copies of the same tape, or different movies of the same girl.

Not that it mattered. Except that if they were multiple copies of the same tape, it meant they weren't merely for home use, but for distribution.

I wasn't sure whether or not this had occurred to Rob yet, and I wasn't about to bring it up. He looked pale enough as it was.

"He's taping them," he said dazedly from where he sat on the closet floor . . . which was carpeted in—what else?—beige.

"Some of them," I said. I'd been relieved there'd been no tapes marked HANNAH. I just hoped the reason why—that the tapes of Hannah, if they existed, were upstairs in 2T—didn't occur to him.

"You don't think he's got tapes of Hannah somewhere?" Rob demanded.

Ooops. So I guess it *had* occurred to him.

"Let's not jump to conclusions," I said.

But it was too late. Rob was already on his feet.

Damn it.

I struggled to put all the videotapes we'd pulled out back into the boxes they'd come from.

"Rob," I said. "Wait. Don't do anything—"

"Don't do anything what?" Rob demanded, whipping around to glare down at me from the closet doorway.

· 145 ·

"Hasty? Violent? What? Jess, what do you want me to do? That's my *sister*."

Then he turned around and stomped from the room.

Damn it again. I shoved all the videos I could grab into the box I was holding, and staggered out after him. I'm not kidding, that box was heavy. There were a lot of videos in it.

"Rob," I called. "Rob, don't—"

But it was too late. He'd left the apartment.

I knew where he was going, though, and I hurried after him, lugging the box of tapes.

"Rob," I said, lurching out into the warm evening air and following him up the outdoor cement steps to the second floor of the apartment complex. "You don't want to do this."

"Actually," he said, as he breezed past 2S, and found himself outside 2T. "I really do."

"Well, at least let me—"

But it was too late. Before I had a chance to take out my ID card, he'd kicked the door open with a single powerful blow from the heel of his motorcycle boot.

"Well," I said, putting down the box of tapes and following him inside, "that was subtle. No one noticed that, I'm sure."

Two-T looked exactly the same as I'd left it a few

hours before. And the setup was exactly the same as it had been in the apartment below. The camera was in the bedroom closet, behind the mirror. Only the names on the videotapes were different. There was, unfortunately, one marked HANNAH.

"That's it," Rob muttered. "He's dead."

"No, he isn't," I said tartly, taking the videotape from his hands and putting it back in the box it had come from. "You aren't going to do anything to him, Rob. I mean it. The police can handle it."

Rob's breathing was on the heavy side. He seemed to be trying to force down something that wouldn't stay put.

"That's what you're going to do with those?" he demanded, thrusting his chin towards the box I was holding. "Hand them over to the police?"

"Eventually," I said. "First, I'm going to watch them."

Rob made an incredulous face. "You're going to—?"

"I have to," I interrupted quickly. "Somebody's got to try to find out what happened to all these girls, don't you think?"

Rob's expression changed. "You think he—?"

Again, I interrupted. "I don't know. But I'm going to find out. And then . . . well, I plan on using them as leverage."

"Leverage?" Now it was Rob's turn to follow me. He trailed after me as I left 2T, putting the box I held on top of the box I'd taken from 1S. "Leverage for what?"

"I'm not sure yet," I said, straightening. "But one thing I do know—this is a lot bigger, Rob, than just one guy shacking up with multiple girls. This looks like it might be a little home-based business Randy's got going on the side, and that's different than if he was just a horny jerk with a penchant for teenage runaways. You see that, don't you?"

Rob's breathing was still pretty heavy. In the quiet evening air, it was all I could hear, aside from the crickets and the occasional laugh track from someone's TV inside their apartment.

The gaze he focused on me in the glare from the outdoor overhead bulb was laser sharp.

"Jess," he said. His voice was laden with suspicion. "What are you doing?"

"Let's not talk about it here," I said as a woman with a golden retriever on a leash came out of 2L and looked at us questioningly before heading down the stairs. "Come on. Grab a box."

Rob—to my surprise—did as I asked . . . only he grabbed both boxes, and started down the stairs.

"Moving out?" the woman asked me pleasantly as we went by her on our way to the parking lot.

"Yeah," I said.

"He's much better looking than your last boyfriend," the woman said with an approving wink, nodding towards Rob's departing back.

"I'm not—" I started to stammer, realizing she thought I lived in 2T with Randy. "He's not—" Then, blushing scarlet, I just said, "Thanks," and hurried to catch up with Rob.

"What did she say?" he asked me as he headed towards his truck.

"Nothing," I said. I hoped he couldn't see how red my face was in the glow from the streetlamps. "Will you follow me home and drop these off with me? I can't take them on my bike."

Rob looked like he wanted to say something, but he just nodded and climbed into his truck, after stowing the boxes in the back. I went to the next parking lot and got my bike—trying not to think about how nice Rob's backside had looked in those faded jeans as he'd climbed into his truck—then cruised over to where he was waiting.

Then we both headed out of the Fountain Bleu apartment complex, and towards my house on Lumbley Lane.

It was a warm summer night in southern Indiana. Downtown, the high school kids were out in full force, tooling up and down Main Street in their parents' cars, and gathered in clusters outside what had been the Chocolate Moose but what was now a Dairy Queen. As I stopped at a red light—had there always been a traffic light there or was that new, too?—and gazed at the kids clutching their Peanut Buster Parfaits, it was hard not to think how young they looked, even though it hadn't been so long ago that I'd been in one of those clusters myself. . . .

Although, now that I thought about it, I hadn't, really. Ever hung out much downtown, I mean. I hadn't had that many friends in high school, aside from Ruth, who'd always been on a diet, anyway. I know how much my mom had longed for me to be like the girls I saw now, swinging their long hair and laughing up in the faces of the clean-cut looking guys who'd brought them there.

But I'd always worn my hair short, and the only boy I'd ever been interested in wasn't exactly one my mom approved of. . . .

"Jess?"

I turned my head. Had someone said my name?

"Jess Mastriani?"

There it was again. I looked around and saw a woman standing on the curb, her arm through the arm of a dark-haired guy in an IZOD and jeans.

"Oh my God, that *is* you!" the woman cried, when I flipped up the glass shield on my helmet to get a better look at her. "Don't you recognize me, Jess? It's me, Karen Sue Hankey!"

I stared at her. It *was* Karen Sue. Only she was looking much, much different than the last time I'd seen her.

Then again, considering the fact that one of the last times I'd seen her, her nose had still been in a splint from when I'd broken it, this wasn't much of a surprise.

Still, she looked totally different than she had in high school. She had done something to straighten her hair, and had ditched her usual frills for a sophisticated sleeveless sheath of some kind, in cream.

And obviously, she'd had her nose done.

"God, I can't believe it's you," Karen Sue enthused. "Scott, look who it is! Jessica Mastriani. You remember, the one I told you I went to high school with? Lightning Girl? The one that television show is based on."

Scott—whom I took to be some kind of frat guy Karen Sue had brought home from whatever Ivy League college she was attending, in order to meet her parents—drawled, "Oh, sure. Jessica Mastriani. I've read all about you, of course, and the incredible things you've done for our country. It's a pleasure to meet you."

I just stared at them. The last time I'd seen Karen Sue—well, close to the last time, anyway—I'd had my fist in her face. And now she was acting like we'd been the best of friends?

This is what happens when you get even a little bit of fame. Everyone—even your sworn enemies—tries to make nice with you.

"You do remember me, don't you, Jess?" Karen Sue didn't look worried. She let out one of her annoying, tinkly laughs. "I'd heard you lost your powers, and all, but nobody said you'd lost your memory! Listen, what are you doing tomorrow morning? Want to have brunch? Maybe we could do some shopping after. Call me. I'm at my parents' for the week. Just visiting down from Vassar."

The light turned green. I flipped my visor down.

"Or I guess I could call you," Karen Sue screamed. *Now* she was looking worried. "You're at your parents' place, right? Jessica? Jess?"

I gunned the engine and took off. Whatever else Karen Sue said was lost in the roar of my muffler.

I didn't slow down again until I'd reached my driveway. I cut the engine and was pulling off my helmet when Rob pulled up alongside me.

"What was that all about?" he wanted to know. "Who was that girl?"

"No one," I said. "Just someone I used to know."

Rob studied me through the open driver's-side window. "Someone you used to know, eh," he said tonelessly. "Guess there're a lot of people around here who you could say that about."

"Guess so," I said, not rising to the bait . . . whatever it was. "Can I have my boxes, please?"

Rob shook his head. But he got out of the truck and went around to get the boxes of tapes, and set them gently on my lawn.

It was quiet on Lumbley Lane, which wasn't exactly a main thoroughfare. There were only a few lights on in Tasha's parents' house across the street, and only a few on in my own house, as well. People in southern Indiana go to bed early—after the eleven o'clock news, at the latest. It's not like in New York, where sometimes the parties don't even start until midnight, or two or three A.M. The only things still up at two or three A.M. in this part of the world were crickets.

"Are you going to let me in on the plan," Rob wanted to know, breaking the evening's stillness, "or are you going to keep on shutting me out?"

I felt my jaw clench. "I'm not the one shutting people out," I said.

"Oh, right." Rob actually laughed at that.

"I'm *not*," I insisted. How dare he laugh? *He* was the one who wouldn't level with me about Miss Boobs-As-Big-As-My-Head. Not that I'd brought her up lately. But still.

"I can't sit around and do nothing about this guy, Jess," Rob said.

"I know that," I said. "And we won't be doing nothing. We're just not going to hurt him. Physically, anyway. Look. You're just going to have to trust me on this."

Which was when he looked down at me and said, an incredulous look on his face, "Oh, right. You mean the way you trust me?"

I knew what was coming then.

And I also knew I was nowhere near ready for it.

"I gotta go," I said, and whirled around to seize one of the boxes and head for my parents' front porch.

But Rob—just as I'd feared he would—slipped out a hand to catch my arm.

"Jess."

His voice, in the still evening air, was gentle . . . though his grip, as I tried to shake it off, was most definitely not.

"I seriously don't want to talk about this right now," I said through gritted teeth, keeping my gaze rooted on my parents' front door. No way was I going to look him in the eye. No *way*. I'd melt if I did. I'd melt into a puddle of tears right there on the lawn.

"We have to talk about it sometime," Rob said in that same gentle voice. But his grip didn't loosen one iota. "I'm not letting you go until we do. Not this time."

"You have to let me go," I said, still keeping my gaze glued to the front door. My mother had painted it blue. When had she done that? It had always been red before. "The paper boy will call the cops in the morning if he gets here and finds us like this."

"I don't mean we have to do it tonight," Rob said. And now he did relax his grip. I yanked my arm away and turned to glare at him. It was safe, I knew, to look at him. So long as he wasn't touching me.

"But we've got to talk about it sometime before you leave to go back to New York," Rob went on. His expression, in the light from the moon that was just beginning to rise, was as serious as I'd ever seen it. "I know you don't want to, but I do. I have to. I don't think I'll ever be able to move on if we don't."

I had to laugh at that one.

"Oh," I said. "You haven't moved on?"

He frowned. "No. What makes you think I have?"

"Gee, I don't know," I said sarcastically. "Maybe it was that blonde I saw you making out with."

The frown deepened. "Jess. I *told* you. That—"

"Jessica! There you are!"

My mother's voice rang out across the lawn.

CHAPTER

13

I turned around to find Mom on the front porch, looking down at us.

"Aren't you going to invite your friend inside?" Mom wanted to know.

Then she flicked the porch light on and saw who "my friend" actually was.

"Oh," she said, startled. "Hello, Robert."

Rob looked as if he tasted something foul. But his voice, when he spoke, was friendly enough. "Hey, Mrs. Mastriani."

"Well," Mom said. "I'm sorry. I didn't realize—I didn't mean to interrupt—"

"It's okay," I said, bending over to retrieve my boxes. I lifted them both without a problem. That's how freaked out I was. I didn't even notice how heavy they were. "You didn't interrupt anything. We were just saying good night."

"Right," I heard Rob say as I hurried to cross the lawn. "We were just saying good night."

"Call me in the morning, Rob," I said, climbing the steps to the porch. "So we can talk about what we're going to do about that *situation*."

"I'll do that," Rob said, behind me. "Good night."

"Good night, Robert," my mother called to him. Then, to me, as I was crossing the porch, she said pleasantly, "What have you got there, Jessica?"

"Just some videotapes," I said, brushing past her and heading into the house in the hopes of getting away before she noticed how red my face was . . . and how hard my heart was slamming into my ribs.

Fortunately, Mom didn't seem to notice how discombobulated I was. She wasn't interested in what was in the boxes I held, either. She was more interested in finding out what was going on between Rob and me.

"Videotapes?" she echoed, closing the front door behind us. Outside, I heard Rob start up his truck. "I see. Well. I didn't know you and Rob Wilkins were back in touch."

"We're not," I said. "Well, not really. We're just . . . we're working on a project together, that's all. Something to do with his sister." I had started towards the door to the basement—my dad had set up a den down there where he could watch sports undisturbed.

"I didn't know Rob had a sister," Mom said.

"Yeah. Well, neither did Rob."

"Oh." My mom had always been able to put more meaning in a single word than anyone I knew. That *Oh* spoke volumes—mostly about how not surprised she was that someone of Rob's ilk would turn out to have an illegitimate sibling.

"And what about that girl?" Mom wanted to know. "That one you said you saw him kissing that day?"

Now more than ever, I wished I'd kept my mouth shut about Miss Boobs-As-Big-As-My-Head. At least where my parents were concerned.

"Was that his sister?" Mom asked.

"God, Mom. No!"

"Oh," Mom said. "Well, what, then? Are you just going to forgive him for that? You were off, risking your life, fighting a war, while he—"

"Mom," I said with a groan. "Knock it off, okay?"

"Well, I'm just saying," Mom went on, "if it happened once, it will happen again. That's the problem with boys like that."

I paused in the basement doorway and looked back at her from over my shoulder.

"Boys like what, Mom?" I asked her in a very quiet voice.

"Well, you know," she said. "Boys who haven't had

the same advantages you had growing up."

"You mean Grits," I said, impressed at how even I managed to keep my tone.

"No, that is not what I mean," Mom said, looking offended. "I'm sure Rob is a very nice young man—his penchant for kissing other girls behind your back aside. But you know perfectly well he's never going to leave this town."

"What's wrong with living in this town?" I demanded. "You and Dad live here. Douglas lives here. If it's good enough for you, why isn't it good enough for me? I mean, for Rob?"

"How can you even ask that?" Mom asked with what I'm positive was genuine wonder. "Jessica, you have so much potential. Why would you want to waste all that staying here in this backwater town, when you could have a real career—travel, meet exciting new people, make a real difference in the world?"

"You know what, Mom?" I said. "I've actually done all that. And look where it got me."

She gave me a sour look.

"You know what I mean, Jessica," she said. "You're a sought-after inspirational speaker, thanks to your former powers and all the good you did with them. Why, I've had letters from groups asking if you'd address their organization from places as far away as Japan. They'd pay all your expenses and as much as twenty thousand dollars in speaking fees. You have a very profitable career ahead of you. . . ."

I looked her dead in the eye—which was kind of hard because I'd started down the steps to the basement and she was standing above me, and she's taller than me under normal circumstances anyway.

"And that's the future you see for me," I said. "Traveling all around the world, talking to people about a power I *used* to have, the good I *used* to do. What about doing good now? Without benefit of my powers? Because there are things I can do now, Mom, that don't involve extrasensory perception."

"Well, of course, sweetheart," my mother said. "All of your professors say you could easily become part of a world-class orchestra if you'd just apply yourself. You could tour the globe, playing in exciting places like Sydney, Australia. And since Skip will probably get a job with an investment firm in New York City, if you got a position with the Philharmonic, why, that would be just perfect! You two could get a little apartment together, and come back to visit us at holidays, and . . . well, who knows? Maybe even get married and start a family of your own!"

I just looked at her. What could I say? I couldn't admit that the thought of being in a world-class orchestra made me want to run screaming down the street. I couldn't admit that I was so sick of traveling, I balled up every single one of those speaking gig requests she forwarded to me, and threw them down the incinerator. I couldn't admit that the thought of marrying Skip made me feel like I'd never stop barfing.

Because if I said any of those things, I know she'd be like, *"Well, then what do you want to do instead?"*

And if I told her, she'd be the one who'd never stop barfing.

So I just said, "Look. I have stuff to do."

And continued down the stairs to the basement.

"Well," Mom said to my departing back. "Don't stay up too late! That nice Karen Sue Hankey called a few minutes ago. She wants to take you to brunch in the morning. I'm so glad you two made up. I never understood why you didn't like Karen Sue. She's such a nice girl."

Great. I rolled my eyes. I was still rolling them when I got down to the basement and found my dad sitting in front of the television, which he'd put on mute, evidently so he could eavesdrop on my conversation with Mom.

"I always thought that Karen Sue girl was a bit of a drip myself," he said to me. "But maybe she's improved with age."

"She hasn't," I assured him, and set down my boxes as Chigger, who'd been sleeping on the couch next to my dad (a definite no-no, in Mom's book), jumped up to give me a lick before settling down again.

"What have you got there?" my dad asked, curious.

"Amateur pornos," I said.

My dad raised his eyebrows. "Interesting. I assume you brought them down here to watch them."

"Just to see if they're for home use or distribution."

"There's a difference?"

"Well, one's protected under the First Amendment," I said. "The other is a crime if the girls are underage and didn't know they were being filmed."

"Actually, if they're underage, I think they're both crimes," Dad said. He lifted his remote and turned off the cable. "Be my guest."

I inserted the first tape and watched as a young girl I assumed was Tiffany—wearing only a bra and panties—flung herself across a bed I recognized as the one in Apartment 1S.

"—though I'm not sure this is exactly what Dr. Phil means when he encourages fathers to spend more time bonding with their daughters," Dad went on.

A man appeared on screen, wearing a pair of tighty-whities. Before anything untoward could occur, I ejected the tape, and inserted the next one titled TIFFANY.

"May I ask where you got these masterpieces of modern cinema," Dad wanted to know, "and who that young man might be?"

"I think he's Randy Whitehead Junior," I said, pressing PLAY.

"Son of wealthy land developer Randall Whitehead Senior," my dad said, sounding impressed, as we watched Tiffany fling herself across the bed in 1S all over again. "Randy's peddling amateur porn now. His father must be so proud."

"I'm not sure his father knows," I said, popping out the tape. It was obviously a copy of the first one we'd seen.

"But why do I have the feeling," Dad said, "that he's going to find out shortly?"

"Because that's the kind of daughter you raised," I said, and popped in a tape marked KRISTIN.

"Be careful, Jess," Dad said. "Randy Whitehead Senior is a pretty powerful guy around here these days. He's rumored to have connections up in Chicago."

"By connections," I said, watching as the dark-haired girl I'd seen Randy kiss outside of 1S appeared on screen, "I'm assuming you mean the Mob?"

"You assume correctly."

"Don't worry," I said, popping out the tape and inserting the next one marked KRISTIN. So that was the dark-haired girl's name. Kristin. Where was Kristin now,

I wondered? Holed up with Randy at his parents' house? He'd have a hard time explaining to them what he was doing with a girl so much younger than he was. "I've got backup."

My dad's face was blank, his tone completely neutral. "So I heard. At least, I thought I overheard your mother mentioning something to you about Rob Wilkins."

"Yeah," I said. The second tape marked KRISTIN was obviously the same as the first one. I pressed EJECT again. "That's why I came back. His sister—it turns out he has a half sister—ran away, and he asked me to help find her."

I don't know why I felt comfortable explaining all this to my dad, but not my mom. I guess it's because my dad had always liked Rob, and Mom . . . hadn't.

"And did you?" Dad asked, again in that carefully neutral tone.

I inserted a new tape. I said, keeping my eyes on the TV screen, "Yes."

"So. It's back."

I didn't have to ask what he meant. I knew what *it* was.

"Yes," I said, still looking at the TV screen, on which a redhead who couldn't have been more than fourteen or fifteen was jumping up and down on the bed—the one in 2T.

"What are you going to do about that?" my dad wanted to know.

"I don't know yet," I said. I ejected the tape as soon as Randy appeared on screen.

"Do these tapes," Dad wanted to know, "have anything to do with Rob's sister?"

My hand hovered over the tapes marked HANNAH. I pulled out one with the redhead's name on it instead.

"Yes," I said. I didn't feel as if I were betraying Rob's confidence in admitting this to my dad. Because he was my dad.

"That's tough," Dad said. "He's gotta be hurting."

"He's not too happy about it," I admitted.

"Unhappy enough to do something stupid to Randy?" Dad asked.

"If I don't stop him," I said.

"Anything happens to Randy," Dad said, "and his father will call in some favors from his friends in Chicago. Rob could find himself in a heap of trouble."

"I know," I said. Although I wasn't as worried about Rob ending up with cement blocks on his feet as I was about him ending up inside a cell block. "I'm working on a plan that will be mutually satisfying to all parties."

"Hmmm," Dad said. "That's a nice change of pace. Usually if a fight were brewing, you'd be the first in line."

"Well," I said. "I've had my fill of fighting."

"That's good to know," my dad said. Then, in a tone that was no longer neutral, but filled with fatherly concern, he added, "Jess, I heard you and your mother up there. Don't let her get you down. You know we'll support you—she and I both—no matter what you decide to do."

And suddenly, my eyes were filled with tears. The images on the screen before me swam.

"I don't want to be a concert flutist, Dad," I heard myself saying.

"I know," was all Dad said.

"And I don't want to go on the lecture circuit and talk about my powers," I told him, not looking away from the blurry TV screen.

"I know."

"And I don't want to marry Skip."

"I wouldn't want to marry Skip, either. But what *do* you want?" Dad asked.

"I want . . ." I sniffled. I couldn't help it. "I don't know what I want. But I can't go back to Dr. Krantz. I *can't*."

"No one's asking you to. And if they do, I think you should say no."

"But how can I, Dad?" I asked, looking at him, finally. Although I couldn't really see him, because of the tears. "Douglas was right. People *need* me."

"They do," my dad said with a nod. "Only I'm not sure they need you in the way that you mean. There are other ways to do good, you know, than the way you've been doing it. And I think you've done more than your share of that. Maybe it's time to try something new."

"But what, Dad?" I asked, my voice cracking.

"Something you actually like doing," Dad said. "Something that makes you happy. Any idea what that might be?"

I tried to think back to the last time I felt happy. Really happy. It was kind of horrible that I couldn't remember. All I could think of was the look on the faces of the kids at Ruth's day camp—the look they gave me when I handed them a shiny flute, donated from some corporation, and told them I could teach them to play it.

"Well," I said slowly. "Yeah. I guess I have an idea."

"Good," Dad said. "Now see if you can figure out a way to do that all the time. That's what life's all about, you know. Finding what it is that you love to do, then doing it as much as you can." He glanced at the television screen. "So long as it's legal, that is."

I reached up to wipe away my tears. I don't know why, since I was no closer to figuring out what I wanted to do with my life. But I felt a little better.

"Thanks, Dad," I said. "That . . . that helps."

"Good," Dad said. And then he stood up. "Well, I don't know about you, but I'm beat. I'm going to bed. I'll leave you to this, if that's all right."

"Okay," I said. "Good night."

"Good night. Oh, and Jessica. About Randall Senior. I don't know if this will help, but it's something that might come in handy."

And then he told me something. Something that made my jaw drop.

Then he said, "Turn the light off when you're through down here. You know how your mom doesn't like us wasting electricity."

And he went upstairs to bed.

CHAPTER
14

When I came downstairs the next morning, it was to find my father—Chigger at his side, as usual—looking out the living room window. The way he was ducking behind the curtain made it clear that whoever it was that he was spying on, he didn't want them to see him looking.

"Let me guess," I said. "Unmarked four-door sedan with tinted windows."

He turned to me, looking astonished. "How did you know?"

"Unbelievable," I muttered, though not in response to his question. I went into the kitchen and found Mom there making scrambled egg whites. Dad's not allowed to have the yolks anymore since his cholesterol checkup.

"Morning, honey," Mom said. "Sleep well?"

Until she'd asked, I hadn't actually thought about it. But the surprising answer was "Yeah, actually. I did."

Not that I hadn't dreamed. I'd dreamed plenty.

And had been on my cell phone all morning because of it.

"I didn't make anything for you," Mom said, "because I know you're going to brunch with that nice Karen Sue Hankey."

"No, I'm not," I said, opening the fridge and peering inside. It was weird to be home and not have either of my brothers around. For one thing, the orange-juice carton was still full. If either Douglas or Mikey had been home, that thing would have been put back empty.

"Oh, honey," Mom said. "You have to go with her. I told her you would."

"Well, you shouldn't make social engagements for me without checking first," I said, opening the carton and drinking from it.

"Oh, Jessica, use a glass," Mom said, looking disgusted. "You aren't on the army base anymore."

Didn't I know it. One good thing about being stationed overseas—if you could call anything about it good—was that no one signed you up to have brunch with Karen Sue Hankey without your permission.

"Tell Karen Sue I'm sorry," I said, putting the carton back in the fridge. "But I've got some errands to run."

"What kind of errands?" Mom wanted to know.

Dad called from the living room, "Jess. Rob just

pulled up out front."

"That kind," I said to Mom. And started for the front door.

"Honey." Mom followed me, ignoring the egg whites sizzling on the stove. "I thought we'd talked about this. That boy is no good for you."

"Bye, Mom," I said, yanking open the front door. Rob was outside, in his shiny black pickup. He waved.

"Hey, Mrs. Mastriani," he called.

"Hello, Robert," my mom called back weakly. To me, she said in a low voice, "Jessica, you know as well as I do, if he cheated once, he'll do it again."

"Toni," my dad said from the chair he'd sunk into in the living room. "Let the kids work out their problems themselves."

"Oh, right," Mom said, whipping around to glare at my father. "I'm just supposed to stand by and let her do whatever she wants, then be here to help pick up the pieces when it all blows up in her face."

"Exactly," Dad said, and flipped open the newspaper.

"Joe!" Mom cried, frustrated.

"See ya," I said to the two of them, and hurried down the porch steps and across the lawn to where the four-door with the tinted windows sat.

After waving at Rob to let him know I'd just be a

minute, I tapped on the sedan's driver's-side window. When it didn't roll down right away, I said, "Come on. We all know you're in there."

Slowly the window came down. I found myself looking at two gentlemen wearing suits, despite the summer heat, which only promised to get steamier.

"Hi," I said to them. "You guys from the FBI, or Mr. Whitehead?"

The two men exchanged glances. Then the driver said in a thick Chicago accent, "Mr. Whitehead. He is not pleased with you. He believes you broke into his son's apartment last night, and took some property belonging to him. Mr. Whitehead would like that property back."

"Right," I said. "I figured he would. Well, it just so happens that my friend and I are on the way to Mr. Whitehead's office. So you two are welcome to follow us. You can even call ahead, if you want, and let him know we're on the way. Oh, and tell him to make sure Randy Junior is there, as well. And Randy needs to bring Kristin with him."

The driver and his partner exchanged glances. I said encouragingly, "Go on. Call him. If he wants his son's property back, he's going to have to meet with me. It's either that, or I take the property to the cops."

The driver hesitated, then reached into his breast

pocket. For a minute, I thought he might be going for a gun, and I thought to myself, obscurely, how odd it would be to die on such a bright, sunny summer morning, on my own street, in front of my parents and my would-have-been boyfriend.

But it turned out he was only reaching for a cell phone.

"See you in ten," I said to the men in the car. Then I turned and started for Rob's truck . . .

. . . just as a white convertible Rabbit pulled up alongside my driveway, and Karen Sue Hankey, behind the wheel, tootled on the horn.

"Hi, Jessica!" she cried. "Are you ready? I hope you don't mind if it's just the two of us, but Scott's playing golf with my dad. I thought it might be just as well. Now it can be just us girls. I made a reservation at that new little gourmet restaurant on the courthouse square. They've got the best waffles. Even though, you know, I'm not supposed to be eating refined sugar. But this is a special occasion. Oh, I just love your hair like that. Did you get it done in New York? Hop in, why don't you?"

Instead of hopping in, I walked right past her car, then climbed into the passenger seat beside Rob.

"Hey," he said to me. Then glanced out his window. "Isn't that that girl from last night? The one who stopped you on the street?"

"Just drive," I said.

Rob obliged, pulling out and heading towards downtown. As we cruised by her, I heard Karen Sue, looking outraged, say, "Well, of all the—" Then I saw my mom rushing out to placate her, probably with an offer of scrambled egg whites.

"How's Hannah?" I asked, buckling my seat belt.

"She hates me," Rob said simply. "She's also not too fond of Chick, whose babysitting her again until her mother gets here to pick her up."

"She'll get over it," I said. "Did you tell her about the videos?"

"Oh, yeah," Rob said. "She doesn't believe me. Her precious Randy would never do anything like that. She thinks I'm making it up to make Randy look bad."

"Of course you are," I said with a laugh. "Don't worry. She'll come around."

"Yeah," Rob said. "Too bad by the time she does, she'll be back home with her mom." He glanced into his rearview mirror a few seconds later. "Who's the tail?" he wanted to know. "FBI?"

"Mob," I said casually. "Turns out Randy Senior's connected."

"Boy," Rob said. "Things just keep getting better with this guy. My sister sure knows how to pick 'em.

Should I lose them?"

"No, they're our escort," I said.

"Great," he said even more sarcastically. "May I ask where this little procession is headed?"

"Absolutely," I said. "Courthouse square. The offices of Mr. Randall Whitehead Senior are in the Fountain Building."

"And that's where we're going?" Rob asked. "To see Randy Senior?"

"That's correct," I said. "Although Randy Junior is going to be there as well, I believe."

"Does this mean you're going to let me beat him senseless after all?" Rob asked hopefully.

"It most certainly does not," I said, keeping my gaze on the road and not allowing it to stray towards Rob's hands, which looked tantalizingly strong and competent as they turned the wheel. I tried not to think about how those hands would feel—had felt—on me.

"Did you watch the tapes?" Rob wanted to know. I noticed he was keeping his own gaze on the road, as well.

"I did," I said.

Rob waited for me to go on. When I didn't, he said, "Were the ones with Hannah . . . I mean, was there more than one—"

"There was just one video of her," I said.

"Good," Rob said softly.

"Multiple copies of the same video," I added, even though I didn't want to. Still, I had to make sure he understood.

Rob swore under his breath. Then, giving a chuckle that was completely devoid of humor, he said, "And you really think I'm not going to kill him when I see him?"

"You're not," I said. "Because, for one thing, he's not worth going to jail for. And for another, those guys back there? They're armed."

"Yeah," Rob said. "Well, they're not going to be around forever. Randy's going to have to go somewhere alone sometime, and when he does—"

"Rob." My voice was sharp enough to cause him to turn his head to look at me, finally.

"You're not going to lay a finger on Randy Whitehead," I said angrily. "You're going to let me handle this. That's what you brought me here from New York for, and that's what I'm going to do."

"Like hell," Rob said. "This is *not* what I brought you from New York for. I brought you from New York to find my sister, and you—"

"There's a spot," I said, pointing. Finding parking around the square was notoriously difficult, which was why so many people preferred to do their shopping at the mall, even though it wasn't anywhere near as historically picturesque.

"—found my sister," Rob went on, swinging the massive truck into the narrow spot as neatly as if he were driving a car half its size. "For which I thank you. But I can't sit back and let this guy get away with what he did to her. I can't do it, Jess. You can't ask me to."

"I'm not," I said, unsnapping my seat belt. "Randy's going to pay for what he did. Just not with his blood. And you're not going to go to jail—or worse, the bottom of some lake."

Rob glared at me. I wouldn't back down, though. I just glared right back. After a few seconds, Rob turned and pounded the sides of his fists on the steering wheel—just once, apparently to get the urge to hit something out of his system.

"Feel better?" I asked.

"No," he said sullenly.

"Good," I said. "Let's go."

We climbed down from the pickup's cab, then waited for the light in order to cross the street to the Fountain Building, which also housed the local bank and a yoga studio. On the way, we passed Underground Comix, the store where my brother Douglas works. The sign in the door read CLOSED. I knew they didn't open until ten, and it was still only nine thirty.

I noticed that when we got to the building's

entrance, the men from the sedan were already waiting for us. They'd apparently found parking closer by.

"Mr. Whitehead in?" I asked them.

The driver, who clearly used Just For Men in order to color his gray, since no one had hair that black, nodded.

"Both Mr. Whiteheads will see you," he said.

"Great," I said chipperly, and led the way through the atrium lobby to the offices of Whitehead Construction.

The plump, middle-aged receptionist must have been given the heads-up that we were on the way, since she didn't ask who we were. Instead she said, jumping up nervously, "Mr. Whitehead will see you right away. Can I get you anything? Coffee? Water? Soda?"

"I'm fine," I said graciously. Who said I didn't learn any manners when I was overseas?

"I'm good," Rob growled.

"Well, then," the receptionist said. "Follow me."

She led us into a large, sunny office, one corner of which was completely taken up by an enormous, modern-looking desk, where Randy Whitehead Senior sat. In front of the desk had been arranged four matching chairs, also modern, made of black leather and chrome. In one of the chairs sat Randy Whitehead Junior. In the other, looking very small but stylish in tight jeans and a black halter top, sat the girl I recognized from Apartment 1S, and later, from the videotapes marked KRISTIN.

"Well, well," Randy Whitehead Senior said, climbing to his feet and putting on a gigantic grin when he saw me. "Are you telling me this little bitty thing here is the one who's been causin' all this ruckus?"

"Her friend's not so little," Randy Junior muttered with a hostile glance in Rob's direction, which Rob ignored.

"Hello, Mr. Whitehead," I said coolly, crossing the office and holding my right hand out towards the senior Randall Whitehead. "I'm Jessica Mastriani. It's very nice to meet you."

"And you, and you," Randy Senior boomed. He pumped my hand up and down, then looked questioningly at Rob, who just stood there, glaring back at him. "Aren't you going to introduce me to your friend?"

"Sure," I said. "Mr. Whitehead, this is Rob Wilkins. Your son, Randy, is acquainted with Rob's younger sister, Hannah."

A glance at Randy Junior told me that the blow had hit home. He'd stood when I entered. Now the younger Mr. Whitehead sank back down into his chrome-and-leather chair, looking up uneasily at Rob, who, even when standing, towered over him by a good four or five inches.

"Oh God," Randy Junior moaned under his breath.

Kristin, noticing her boyfriend's pale demeanor, chimed in with, "Who's Hannah? What's going on, Randy? Who's Hannah?"

"I'll tell you later," Randy Junior muttered.

"You must be Kristin," I said to the dark-haired girl and held out my hand. "Jessica Mastriani."

"Oh," she said, bewilderedly putting out her own hand. "You're a friend of Randy's? He's told you about me?"

"Not exactly," I said. "I've seen your video."

"Video?" Kristin looked puzzled. "What video?"

I glanced at Randy Senior and noticed that his smile lost some of its strength.

"Oh, you don't know about the video Randy made of you and him in bed together?" I asked. "The one he's distributing all over southern Indiana, and—if I'm not mistaken, across state lines . . . which is a felony, I think."

Kristin laughed, a tinkling sound in the quiet office, the walls of which were decorated with framed aerial photos of famous golf courses. "Randy and I never made a video," she said. "What's she talking about, Randy?"

"All righty, then," Randy Senior interrupted in that same booming voice. "I understand from my son here, Miss Mastriani, that you stole some property of his. And apparently you confirmed this fact to my two associates here—" He nodded towards Just For Men and his companion, who'd taken up positions flanking the office door, as if they suspected Rob and I might make a run for it. "I'll admit I wasn't completely aware of the extent of Randy's little enterprise until last night when he explained it to me. I take it this all has something to do with this young man's sister?"

He looked questioningly at Rob.

"My *underage* sister," Rob pointed out in a voice so cold, I was surprised it didn't freeze Randy Senior to the spot.

Instead of freezing, the older Mr. Whitehead took a deep breath, then slowly lowered himself back into his chair.

"I see," he said thoughtfully. "That *is* unfortunate." Then, noticing that Rob and I were still standing, Randy Senior said, "Where are my manners? Sit down, you two, please."

Rob stayed where he was, but I sat down, then reached up and tugged on the back of Rob's shirt until he lowered himself into the chair next to mine.

Kristin, meanwhile, kept saying, "Randy? What's going on? Who's this Hannah person? Why is that man there so angry? What are these videos they keep talking about?"

"Miss Mastriani," Randy Senior said in the same affable tone as before, "before we go any further, I have to tell you how truly honored I am to meet you. When Randy here told me he'd met Lightning Girl—the one that television show is based on—well, you could have knocked me over with a feather. For one thing, that show is one of my wife's favorites—right, Randy?"

Randy Junior, who still looked as if he might throw up on his own shoes at any second, said, "Yeah. Right."

"And for another, well, I can't tell you how much I appreciate everything you did for this country during your tour in Afghanistan. That's the kind of sacrifice only a true patriot would make, and Randy's mother and I—well, if there's one thing we admire, that's patriotism. Love for this great country of ours is something we tried to instill in our son—didn't we, Randy? I mean, where else but in America could the son of a dirt-poor farmer like myself end up owning more property than anyone in this great state with the exception of the Catholic Church?"

Randy Senior laughed heartily at his own joke, and Just For Men and his friend joined in. I smiled politely. Rob continued to glower. Randy kept on looking sick, and Kristin just looked confused.

"And I'd like to add," Randy Senior said, when he'd

recovered from his laughing fit, "that the wife and I are big fans of your father's restaurants. Why, we eat at least one meal a week at Mastriani's. And I'm addicted to the burgers at Joe's. Aren't I, Randy?"

Randy nodded, still looking as if he didn't feel well. I said, "Well, that's all just great, Mr. Whitehead. But that doesn't get us any closer to resolving the situation we have here. Your son's behavior has upset my friend here very much. I mean, his sister is a very young, inexperienced girl. And your son not only violated her—"

"I did not," Randy Junior cried. "She wasn't even a virgin when I met her!"

Rob started up from his chair, but before he could lay his hands on Randy Junior, Randy Senior thundered, "Shut up, Randall!"

"But, Dad," Randy Junior cried. "I didn't—"

"You shut up," Randy Senior bellowed, looking very red in the face, "until I tell you different. I think you've caused enough trouble for one day, don't you?"

Randy Junior cowered in his seat, alternating nervous glances between his father and Rob.

Mr. Whitehead looked at me and said, "I apologize for my son's outburst there, Miss Mastriani, and Mr.— I'm sorry, young man, I didn't catch your name."

"Wil—" Rob began, but I cut him off.

"His name doesn't matter," I said quickly. "As I was saying, the fact is, your son violated his sister's right to privacy by filming, without her knowledge, private acts on video, that he then went on to copy and distribute—"

"I had her permission!" Randy Junior cried. "I got her signature on a release form and everything!"

"But that's not a binding contract," I said to his father. "Since Hannah is only fifteen years old—"

"She told me she was eighteen!" Randy Junior burst out, causing his father to lift a crystal golf-ball–shaped paperweight from the top of his desk and then lower it, with a crash, against his blotter.

"God damn it, Randy!" he roared. "I told you to shut up!"

Randy Junior closed his mouth. Beside him, Kristin looked ready to burst into tears. She wasn't the only one, either. Randy Junior looked close to letting loose with a few sobs as well.

"I'm sorry, Miss Mastriani," Randy Senior, recovering himself, said. "And that apology extends to you, too, young man. I can perfectly understand your outrage. I myself am outraged. I had no idea that my son was engaging in the—ahem—film business. I am as disgusted by it as I'm sure you are. So please tell me, what can I do to make this up to you—to both of you? Because I surely do want to set things right."

"Well," I said, "in that case, you can ask your son to turn himself in to the officers who should be waiting in your reception area right about"—I glanced at my watch and saw that it was ten o'clock—"now."

CHAPTER

15

Both Randys were busy gaping at me when the intercom on Mr. Whitehead's desk suddenly buzzed.

Randy Senior snatched at it and barked, "God damn it, Thelma, I said no interruptions during this meeting!"

"I'm sorry, Randy," the receptionist's voice crackled. "But there are about a half dozen police officers out here who say they need to see you right away."

All of the color drained from Mr. Whitehead's face. He looked at me with more venom than a rattler.

"You conniving little bitch," he said.

I smiled at him pleasantly.

Just For Men and his companion had both whipped out cell phones and were whispering urgently into them. Randy Junior had sunk so low into his chair, he looked as if he were boneless. Randy Senior had taken a bottle of Mylanta from a desk drawer and was measuring out a capful of the chalky white liquid. Only Kristin was glancing around confusedly, going, "I don't understand. Why are the police here? Who is this Hannah person? And why does everyone keep talking about videotapes?"

I looked at her and said, "Your boyfriend has been secretly filming the two of you in bed together, then selling the tapes over the Internet on amateur porn sites."

Kristin knit her pretty brow. "No, he hasn't."

"Yes," I said. "He has."

"No," Kristin said with a smirk, "he hasn't. And I think I would know. I mean, I'd have noticed a camera in the bedroom."

"The camera was hidden in the bedroom closet," I said. "Behind the mirror—which was really two-way glass—over the dresser."

Kristin blinked her heavily mascaraed eyelashes. Then she said, "Nuh-uh."

"Uh-huh," I said. "Kristin. I've seen the tapes. You're wearing a matching red tiger-stripe-bra-and-panty set. You also," I added, "have a tendency to giggle."

Kristin went pale beneath her blusher. Her head swiveled towards Randy Junior.

"How would she know that?" she demanded shrilly of her boyfriend. "How does she know that?"

"Because I've seen the tapes, Kristin," I said. "I've seen *all* the tapes. Carly. Jasmine. Beth."

Quick as lightning, Kristin's hand whipped out,

meeting with Randy Junior's face with crackling force.

"You told me Jasmine was your sister," she hissed, tears of fury standing on the ends of her dark eyelashes.

"That's funny," I said as Randy Junior tried to shrink into a ball in his chair. "That's what Jasmine says he told her about you, Kristin."

Kristin swung an astonished gaze towards me. So did Randy Junior. So, for that matter, did Rob.

"You talked to Jasmine?" Randy Junior breathed.

"Oh," I said calmly. "I talked to them all this morning, Randy. And you know, I have to say, even though you made sure to select such a wide variety of different girls—blondes, brunettes, redheads, short, skinny, tall—they all had one thing in common. And that was that they didn't know they were being filmed. And they're all pretty pissed off about it. Most of them pissed off enough to press charges."

"Oh, sweet Lord," Randy Whitehead Senior said, dropping his balding head into his hands.

Randy Junior, meanwhile, had curled into the smallest ball he could. He had to, if he wanted to escape Kristin's slaps, which she was raining down on him with feminine fury.

"You jerk!" she cried. "You lied to me! You lied! You said you loved me! You said I was the only one! You said you'd always take care of me! Where am I going to go now? Huh? Where?"

"You could go home," I suggested quietly.

This caught her attention. She stopped slapping Randy long enough to glance my way.

"No, I can't," she said with a sniffle. "My dad kicked me out."

"He's willing to let you come back," I said. "At least, he was when I spoke to him this morning."

"You . . . you talked to my dad?" Kristin asked as if she didn't dare believe it.

"If you're Kristin Pine from Brazil, Indiana," I said, "then yeah, I did. Your dad was pretty relieved to hear from me, as a matter of fact. He and your mom have been worried about you. Well, who wouldn't worry," I added with a glance at Mr. Whitehead Senior, "about their runaway fifteen-year-old?"

"Christ," Randy Senior said, burying his face more deeply into his hands.

"How . . . how did you know?" Kristin breathed, staring at me incredulously. "Who my parents were . . . who *I* was?"

"She's Lightning Girl," Rob said simply.

I glanced in his direction. I wouldn't say he'd spoken with extreme bitterness, or anything. But he hadn't exactly sounded thrilled. He was sitting back in his chair, sort of just taking the drama in as it unfolded in front of him. He seemed almost relaxed. Well, more so than anyone else in the room.

At least until Randy Whitehead Senior said to me in a voice that was deathly quiet, "You're going to regret this, girlie. I know you did it to get back at my boy for what he did to your friend's sister. But dragging in all those other girls and the police . . . you're going to regret it."

Now Rob didn't look relaxed at all. He leaned forward in his chair and said, "Excuse me. But are you *threatening* her?"

"Oh, you're damned straight I'm threatening her," Randy Senior said. "Her. You. Her parents. This is war, girlie. You crossed the wrong man, this time."

"I don't think so," I said matter-of-factly. "And here's why. The only person going down here today is your son. If anything happens to me, or to my family or friends, you're going to be joining your son in the big house. Or, in your case, I guess you'd call it the dog-house."

Randy Senior blinked at me.

"Just what in the hell," he said, "are you talking about?"

"Well, as the owner and developer of the Fountain Bleu apartment complex, you are, of course, ultimately responsible for the management of it, including who you employ to run it. . . . In this case, that would be your son, Randy, who, as we know now, took advantage of his position there to illicitly house underage runaways, then film them in sex acts with himself—" Across from me, Kristin let out a sob. "Sorry," I said to her apologetically.

"It's okay," she said with a sniff.

I went on. "Obviously, this leaves you pretty open to both criminal and civil charges. You're in a very vulnerable situation right now."

Mr. Whitehead Senior stared at me. "Just what, exactly, are you saying? Are you trying to offer us some kind of deal?"

The buzzer on the intercom sounded again. "Mr. Whitehead." Thelma sounded tense. "I don't know how much longer these police officers are willing to wait on you. . . ."

Randy Senior threw Just For Men and his friend an appealing look. "Go on out there," he said. "And see if you can stall them."

Just For Men nodded. "Will do," he said. And they both left.

Randy Senior looked at me. "Now. Just what kind of deal are we talking about?"

"Oh, no deal for your son," I said quickly. "Obviously. But for you . . . well, there's a piece of property I know you have your eye on—Pine Heights Elementary School?"

Mr. Whitehead's eyes narrowed at me. "That's right. You were at the city council meeting last night. That's where Randy said he met you."

"Right. Your plan is to convert the building to condos. If, however, you could see your way to abandoning the condo plan and put your support—and a sizable donation—towards establishing an alternative school there, I think I might be able to work out a deal with the offended parties that will keep you out of jail and civil court as well."

Randy Whitehead Senior stared at me. So did his son. So did Rob. The only person in the room, in fact, who was not staring at me was Kristin, and that's because she was looking at her reflection in her compact mirror and carefully wiping away the mascara tracks her tears had made down her cheeks.

"Just how much," Randy Senior wanted to know, "of a donation are we talking about here?"

"Oh, nothing much," I said. "To a man of your wealth, anyway. And you could write it off as a tax deduction, I'm sure."

His voice was cold. "How. Much."

"I think three million dollars would work," I said.

Down crashed the golf-ball paperweight again.

Kristin jumped, with a little hiccup.

"There is no way!" Randy Senior bellowed. "No way! Just who in the hell do you think—I have friends in this town, girlie. I'll take my chances in court! I'll pay off whoever I have to! I'll—"

Rob stood up. He was so tall and broad-shouldered that he seemed to take up an astonishing amount of space in the large office.

"You'll do," he said in a deep, quiet voice, "what she tells you to do."

Randy Whitehead Senior made a mistake then. He looked up into Rob's face, and he laughed.

"Oh, yeah?" he squawked. "Or what?"

A split second later, Rob had pulled Mr. Whitehead halfway across his desk, and had the golf-ball–shaped paperweight pressed against his carotid artery.

"Or I'll kill you," Rob replied with no change in tone.

Which is when Randy Senior made his second mistake. He gurgled, "Do you know who I am? Do you know who I know? I can have you snuffed out like a candle, fella."

"Not if you're already dead," Rob said calmly, pressing the golf ball so deeply into Mr. Whitehead's throat that he began to choke.

I got up from my chair and strolled towards

Mr. Whitehead's desk. His face had gotten very red. Beads of sweat were popping out all over his shiny forehead. He rolled his eyes towards me. One hand reached limply for the intercom. But even if he could have reached it, it wouldn't have done any good. He couldn't speak with the pressure Rob was putting on his larynx.

"You may know people in this town, Mr. Whitehead," I said. "But the fact is, Rob here probably knows more. And the people he knows are local. He doesn't need to send all the way to Chicago for muscle. So let's put aside the physical threats for the moment, because the fact is, you're going to do as I say, and not because if you don't, Rob will kill you. You're going to do as I say because if you don't, I'm going to tell your wife about Eric."

Randy Junior looked up from the twitching ball he'd rolled himself into.

"Who's Eric?" he asked tearfully.

Kristin, who'd put away her compact and was staring, transfixed, at the way Rob's muscles were bunched beneath his shirt sleeves (I'd have a word with her about that later), looked equally confused. "Who's Eric?" she wanted to know.

"Yeah," Rob said, looking down at me. "Who's Eric?"

"Okay!"

We all glanced at Mr. Whitehead, surprised he'd been able to summon up an intelligible word.

But he was gripping Rob's hands with white-tipped fingers and croaking, "Okay. Okay."

Rob loosened his hold, and Randy Senior sagged against his desk, gasping for air.

"Okay you'll do what she says?" Rob asked him cautiously.

Mr. Whitehead nodded. His face was slowly turning back to its normal color. "I'll do as she says," he wheezed. "Just don't . . . tell my wife . . . about Eric."

"Fine," I said. "But you should know, I'm not the only one who knows about Eric, Mr. Whitehead. And if anything should happen to me, my associates will—"

"Nothing will happen to you," Mr. Whitehead said. He'd gone almost as pale as he'd been red just moments before. "I swear it. Just don't tell."

"Deal," I said. And I reached across the desk to slip my right hand in his sweaty, trembling one.

Then I leaned down and pushed the button on the intercom.

"Say it," I said to Mr. Whitehead.

He coughed a few times, then adjusted his collar and tie where Rob's grip had mussed them. Then he said into the intercom, "You can send the police in for Randy Junior now, Thelma."

That caused his son to spring from his seat, looking panic-stricken.

"No!" he cried. "Dad! You can't—"

"I'm sorry, Randy," Randy Senior said. And the funny thing was, he really did sound sorry. "But I don't have a choice."

"But I did it for you, Dad," Randy pleaded. "To show you I could handle more responsibility. You can't let them do this! You can't!"

But Mr. Whitehead just stood there as the police who'd come into his office instructed Randy Junior to put his hands up against the wall and proceeded to frisk him.

The police weren't the only ones who came in, either. They were followed by a young guy in a Hellboy T-shirt, brandishing an X-Men comic book.

"Oh, hey, Jess," Douglas said when he saw me. "How'd I do? Did I get 'em here on time, like you asked?"

"*Perfect* timing, Doug," I said. "Perfect timing."

CHAPTER
16

When we emerged from the DA's office several hours later—I had a lot of explaining to do, it turned out, as to exactly how I'd come across the videos I'd given to Douglas to give to them. But they hadn't kept me nearly as long as they seemed to plan on keeping Kristin, who was their star witness and who was being kept in protective custody until her parents could come to pick her up—I was famished enough almost to wish I'd taken Karen Sue up on her offer of brunch. I thought I might pass out on the courthouse steps.

Fortunately Rob seemed to feel the same way, since he went, "What would you say to some lunch?"

"I'd say hallelujah. Douglas?"

Douglas shook his head. "Sorry, no can do. I gotta get back to the shop. Someone's got to make sure that the graphic-novel needs of this community are met." The noon sun was pelting down on us, but I still saw

Douglas's gaze slide towards me. "But you guys go on ahead. You know, there's a really nice place Tasha and I have been going lately, out by Storey, Indiana, that's completely worth the drive. It's right next to this river, and real romantic—"

I knew what he was doing. I knew what he was doing, and I hurried to put a stop to it by pointing across the square. "Oh, look. Joe's is open. We could stop by there and pick up some burgers and take them back to your place, Rob."

Rob raised his eyebrows. "My place?"

"She's the only one on the tapes," I said, "I haven't spoken to yet. I need to know if she wants to press charges against Randy as well. I gave all the other girls the choice."

"You didn't give the cops her tape?" Rob asked, looking curious.

"Not yet," I said.

Rob glanced at his watch. "Gwen'll be there to pick her up any minute. Guess we could get a burger for her, too. And about eight more on top of that, for Chick."

"Or," Douglas said, looking disappointed. "I guess you could do that instead."

"We will," I said firmly. "Thanks for your help this morning, Douglas. We couldn't have done it without you."

He perked up a bit at hearing this. "My pleasure," he said. "Anything to rid the world of more smut-peddlers, and make room for wholesome entertainment like *Sin City.* You two have fun now. Call me later, Jess."

And with a jaunty salute, Douglas started across the street for Underground Comix. He'd doubtless track me down and demand an explanation when he learned about Mr. Whitehead's "donation"—Randy Senior was supposed to present the check personally to the head of the Pine Heights Alternative School committee, which was Douglas himself.

In the meantime, I was glad to have him out of my hair. I didn't exactly need my big brother hanging around, trying to play matchmaker. Things between Rob and me were awkward enough without interference from my family—even though I knew Douglas meant well.

Still, I was totally willing to take advantage of *some* of my family. . . . The nice thing about having parents who own all the best restaurants in town is that you don't have to pay to eat there. Even so, Rob insisted on leaving a hefty tip for our burgers . . . which I understood, considering the fact that his mom used to be one of our waitresses. Burgers bagged and in hand, we got back into his pickup and started for his house.

The silence that ensued in the cab on the way to Rob's wasn't at all awkward. Not. We hadn't had a single moment to ourselves in order to discuss what had happened in Randy Senior's office, because we'd been too busy explaining to the DA what Randy Junior had done. I really didn't think there was all that much to talk about, anyway.

Rob seemed to disagree, though.

"So," he said as we hurtled past cornfields—the corn was only knee-high. In another month, it would be well past the top of my head. "This new nonviolence thing you've got going . . ."

I let out an inward groan. I didn't want to have to explain to Rob—to anyone, for that matter—why it was that hitting no longer held any appeal to me. I'd seen enough violence to last me a lifetime, and I'd hung up my (figurative) brass knuckles. Why couldn't we just leave it at that?

But to my surprise, he finished with ". . . I like it."

I glanced at him. He kept his gaze on the road.

"Yeah," I said sarcastically. "I bet you do. Since your block was one of the first ones I was going to knock off, as soon as I got the chance."

He still wouldn't look at me.

"That's not why," he said. "I just think you're good at thinking up nonviolent solutions to your problems. Like that thing today, back in Whitehead's office. That was genius."

I felt my cheeks heating up, and uttered a silent curse at myself. Why did I let this guy get under my skin? I mean, I was actually blushing, just because he'd given me a compliment. Why did he have this insufferable power over my body temperature?

"I always told you," he went on, still not looking in my direction. Which was good, because if he had, he'd have seen my face heated up red as a lobster. "That the problem with your being so quick with your fists was that someday, someone bigger than you was going to hit you back. And you weren't going to like it very much."

"That would never have happened," I said, trying to keep my tone light. "I'm too quick on my feet. Float like a butterfly—"

"Yeah, well, I think both Randy Whiteheads would agree that your sting is much worse when you use your head," he interrupted, "than your right hook. Who's Eric?"

I blinked at him. "Who?"

"Eric." We'd reached the long driveway to his house, and Rob turned the truck up it. It really was a beautiful piece of land—the one Rob's farm sat on—complete with stately hundred-year-old oaks and its own stream. Randy Whitehead Senior, I'm sure, would have enjoyed turning it into a golf course or country club. "The guy you said you'd tell Mrs. Whitehead about if her husband didn't do what you said."

"Oh," I said with a grin. "Him. Yeah. My dad told me about him. Eric's a waiter at Mastriani's."

"So?"

"So you know how people who work together get to chatting. Eric, my dad says, likes to hang out at a gay bar in Indianapolis."

"Yeah. And?"

"And it turns out, so does Randy Senior."

Rob brought the truck to a stop with a jerk, his foot landed on the brake so fast. Finally he turned his head to look at me.

"You're kidding me," he said, looking stunned.

"Nope." I undid my seat belt and started to climb from the pickup. "In fact, Eric and Mr Whitehead know each other pretty well. They have their own apartment together and everything. Except, apparently, Randy Senior would rather his wife not know about it."

I gathered up all the burgers and started towards Rob's house. Chick—owner and proprietor of Chick's Bar and Motorcycle Club, out by the highway—apparently heard us pull up, since he came to the front door. When he saw me coming up the brick walk, he broke out into an enormous smile.

"Well, if it isn't Lightning Girl," he said, holding open the screen door to let me in. "Long time no see."

"Hi, Chick," I said, grinning back at him. "How's life?"

"A whole lot better now that you're back in town," Chick said as Rob followed me up the walk. "Hey, now that you two are back together, maybe you can do something to make this guy stop working so hard and have some fun once in a while."

Chick slapped a heavy hand down onto Rob's shoulder. Rob winced. But not, I'm pretty sure, because Chick's grip hurt.

"Yeah," Rob said, not looking at me *or* Chick. "Well, Jess came back, but only to help me find Hannah. She'll be heading back to New York soon."

Chick's smile vanished. "Oh," he said. Then he noticed the bags in my hands, and his crestfallen demeanor brightened again, but only slightly. "Well, at least she brought food."

And he started back inside the house.

I turned to glare at Rob. "How do you know?" I demanded.

He stared down at me, confused. "How do I know what?"

"How do you know when I'll be heading back to New York?" I couldn't explain why I suddenly felt so incredibly angry. But I was definitely rethinking my whole nonviolent stance, as well as my decision not to knock his block off. "Maybe I won't be going back to New York. You don't know. You don't know anything about me anymore."

He blinked at me. "Okay," he said. "Take it easy."

Why is it that whenever anyone tells you to *take it easy* or *relax*, it has the totally opposite effect?

Feeling exceptionally unrelaxed, I stomped into Rob's house to find his sister, Hannah, just coming down the stairs to see who was at the door.

"Oh," she said, looking distinctly disappointed when she saw who it was. "It's you. I thought it might be my mom."

"Yeah, well, I'm just as thrilled to see you," I snapped. "Is there a VCR up there?"

Hannah cocked her head quizzically at me from the staircase. "What? Yeah. Why?"

I signaled for her to turn around and head back up the stairs. Rob, going into the kitchen to get plates for the burgers, said, "Jess. Eat first, okay?"

"Oh, Hannah and I are going to eat," I assured him. Then, seeing that Hannah had stayed where she was, I pointed up the stairs again and said, "Go. Now."

Looking churlish, Hannah spun around and headed up the stairs. I followed, after handing Chick all but one of the bags I carried.

Upstairs, in the guest bedroom where Hannah was staying—the one that used to be Rob's, but which he'd done over in muted beige—I saw that she'd made herself at home. Her clothes were strewn all over the floor, along with several bags of chips and numerous empty soda cans.

"You'd better pack," I said to her. "Your mom's on her way to get you, you know."

"I don't care," Hannah said, flopping back onto the bed and glaring at the ceiling. Her multicolored hair made a rainbow against the white pillowcase. "I'm not going back to live with that bitch. And Rob can't make me."

"Uh," I said, pressing POWER on the VCR and inserting the videotape I'd removed from my backpack. "Yes, he can. He is under no obligation to keep paying for you to live under his roof."

"Fine," Hannah said to the ceiling. "He can kick me out, then. He can't make me stay with Mom, though. I'll just run away again."

"Because that worked out so great for you last time?" I pressed PLAY, then took the bag of burgers and went to sit in an armchair by the room's single window—after first removing a pile of Hannah's clothes from it. "Good plan."

Hannah was watching me, not the TV. "Hey," she said, sitting up, "can I have one of those? I'm starved. That Chick guy offered to make me a sandwich, but have you ever looked at his fingernails? I was, like, no way."

After taking a burger out for myself, I tossed the bag to her. "Be my guest." I looked at the TV screen. "Oh, cool," I said, sinking my teeth into the thick cheese-and-bacon combo. "This is my favorite part."

Idly, Hannah glanced up from the burger she was biting into to the TV . . .

. . . then let the burger drop to her lap.

"What?" She stared, bug-eyed, at the screen. "Where did—hey, that's—"

I swallowed. "Yeah. I prefer boxers, too. But what can you do? Some guys will never learn."

Hannah scrambled off the bed—sending burger everywhere—and dove for the VCR. She slammed the EJECT button. When the videotape slid out of the machine, she wrenched it up and stared at the side, where the neatly typed label—HANNAH—caused her eyes to bug out even more.

"Where did you get this?" she demanded in a small voice.

"From your boyfriend's closet," I said when I was done chewing. "You didn't know you were being filmed?"

She shook her head. The ability to speak had apparently left her.

"He had copies, too," I went on. "I assume for distribution purposes."

"Dis . . . distribution?" Hannah's face had gone as white as the sheets behind her. "He was . . . selling them?"

"Oh, not just yours," I said. "There were lots of different tapes of lots of different underage girls. He apparently had quite a little harem going. You really didn't know?"

She shook her head again, staring down at the tape.

"Well," I said with a shrug. "You don't need to worry about it anymore. He's in jail now. Or will be until his dad bails him out, anyway. Unless they hold him without bail, like the DA is threatening. Interstate porn trafficking is actually taken pretty seriously, especially when it involves minors, but Mr. Whitehead—Randy's dad—has a lot of money and power and . . . well. We'll just have to see what happens."

Hannah looked at me. She had a ketchup smear on one side of her mouth. She actually appeared, for the first time since I'd met her, much younger than her fifteen years.

"Randy's in jail?" she asked softly.

"Randy," I said, "is very much in jail. You can help keep him there by letting me give your tapes to the police, and agreeing to testify against him. Which I very much urge you to do. But I guess I'd understand if you chose not to. Though it's not a course I'd recommend. I mean, if he gets away with it, he'll just do it to someone else, maybe even younger than you."

I waited for her to light into me, the way she had back in Randy's apartment. I was, after all, now doubly her enemy—I'd taken her away from the man she loved, *and* now I'd been instrumental in putting that man in jail.

So, of course, had her brother. But I was willing to take the blame for Randy's incarceration, since if Rob had had his way, all her boyfriend would currently be suffering from right now was a concussion, not years of legal woes and quite possibly a good deal of jail time.

But to my surprise, Hannah didn't fly into one of her rages. Instead, still gazing down at the tape, she asked softly, "Did Rob see it?"

I shook my head. "No. Just me."

"Where are the others?" she asked. "You said there were copies."

I reached for my backpack, and pulled out the other two tapes with her name on them.

"Right here," I said.

She stepped forward and took both the tapes from my hand. As she did so, our fingers brushed, and she said in the same soft voice, "Thanks." She looked down at the tapes. And appeared to come to a decision, if the way her mouth turned into a flat little line was any indication.

"I guess I'd like to," she said. "Press charges, I mean."

"Good for you," I said. "Let Rob know. Or your mom. One of them can take you down to the station."

"I will. And . . . I'm sorry."

I raised my eyebrows. "What for? It's not your fault."

"No, not for Randy," she said, keeping her gaze on the tapes. "For those things I said yesterday. About you being—"

"A huge, giant, überbitch?" I finished for her.

"Uh," she said. And she actually blushed. "Yeah. That. You're not. You're actually pretty cool."

"Well," I said. "Thanks."

And then we both heard Rob call up the stairs, "Hannah? Your mom's here."

And Hannah's face crumpled.

"Mom?" She dropped all three videotapes down on the bed, turned around, and ran for the door. "Mom!"

A few seconds later, I heard her thumping down the stairs, and a woman's voice say, "Oh, Hannah!" before she was interrupted by youthful, joyous screaming.

I stayed where I was, finishing the rest of my burger. When I was done, I got up, threw the wrapper in the trash, and started for the door.

But I stumbled and nearly lost my balance when my foot caught on something hidden beneath the detritus on the floor. When I looked down to see what it was, I saw a piece of paper with my name on it. So of course I had to stoop down for a closer look.

The paper turned out to be sticking out of an album—green leather with gold-embossed trim. When I picked it up, it was heavy. More paper came out of it. I saw that they were newspaper clippings, and that they'd come loose due to someone's rough handling.

Someone who, I didn't doubt, had thrown the album across the room in a fit of pique at me.

I had a pretty good idea who that someone was.

And when I opened it, I saw why she'd done it.

CHAPTER
17

It was all about me. Every page in the album—and there were a lot of them, messily inserted and sloppily glued, even before Hannah had inflicted it with such bodily harm. . . . The work of someone not used to scrapbooking and with no interest in neatness or even in using the correct kind of adhesive, Rob seemingly having grabbed whatever was handy, including duct tape—was plastered with magazine and newspaper articles about me, starting from the very first story that appeared in our local paper and progressing to a piece that had appeared in *The New York Times* after the start of the war on terror, on some of the unorthodox methods the government was using to combat terrorism.

There was even the *People* magazine article—the one I'd refused to take part in—about me and my family ("*Though she's the inspiration for a hit television show, Jessica Mastriani is surprisingly camera shy. . . .*").

There weren't just clippings, either. There were some photos, too. I recognized a few of them—snapshots Rob's mother had taken of us at Thanksgiving dinner . . . even a picture of Ruth and me sitting on Santa's lap in the mall, giggling like mad. Rob must have talked the photographer into letting him buy a copy of that one, since I know I hadn't given him one.

But some of the photos I'd never seen before—like a black-and-white one of me, in the center of the book, looking off in the distance, seemingly unaware I was being photographed. I didn't know where or when that photo had been taken, let alone who'd pressed the shutter.

The final thing in the book was the last piece ever written about me—an announcement in our hometown paper of my winning the scholarship to Juilliard. My mom must have submitted that. She'd been so proud—prouder that I'd won that scholarship than she'd been of any of the other things I'd done, or all the kids and fugitives from justice I'd found.

I guess I could understand that. My musical gift was much easier to accept than my other one.

The one that, until recently, I'd thought I'd lost for good.

I could understand my mom keeping an album like this. In fact, she had one just like it.

But that's because my mom loves me—even if we do have our differences.

The question was, why did *Rob* have an album like this—one he'd obviously kept up with, even after we'd parted ways? What did it mean? Obviously that he'd kept on thinking of me, even after I was long gone out of his life. . . .

But had he kept on thinking of me because he loved me? Or had he kept this album as a sort of trophy he could brag about—*I dated Lightning Girl.*

But wouldn't my letters and e-mails to him—the ones I wrote so sporadically while I was overseas—make better material for bragging? And none of those were in the album.

There was only one way I was ever going to find out what it meant. And that was to ask its creator.

Holding the album to my chest—in the hope, I guess, that it would hide the violent hammering of my heart, though why my pulse should be racing so hard was a question I didn't dare ask myself—I left the spare room and came down the stairs to find Hannah and a woman I assumed to be her mother huddled together on the couch in the living room. Both of them were weeping, and speaking to each other in hushed voices.

Chick sat at the dining room table, eating what appeared—if the empty wrappers in front of him were any indication—to be his third cheeseburger. There was no sign of the owner of the house.

"Where's Rob?" I asked Chick, since Hannah and her mother seemed otherwise occupied.

"He couldn't take all the oestrogen," Chick replied with his mouth full. I couldn't help noticing that he seemed to be keeping his eye not on Hannah, but on her mother, who was an attractive blonde around his own age, though considerably slimmer. "He went out to his workshop in the barn."

"Thanks," I said, and started for the door . . .

. . . only to be stopped by Hannah, who cried, "Oh, there she is!" and leaped up to grab my wrist.

"This is her, Mom," Hannah said, dragging me over to where her mother sat on the couch. "Jessica Mastriani. She's the one who found me."

Mrs. Snyder, Hannah's mom, looked up at me tearfully. "I can't thank you enough," she gushed, "for bringing my daughter home."

"Oh, it was nothing," I said. I always did hate this part. "It's very nice to meet you. I have to go now. . . ."

"That's not all she did, Mom," Hannah began, and she started chattering about Randy and his misdeeds, and the part I'd played in getting his no-good butt hauled off to jail, and how she needed to go down to the station house to do her part to keep him there.

Fortunately I managed to wrestle my wrist free and escape without her seeming to notice. A second later, I was out in the bright sunshine, heading for Rob's workshop in the barn.

In the same way that his house had undergone a renovation since the last time I'd seen it, so had Rob's barn. New wood panels lined the walls, so that in winter the place would stay snug, and in the summer, the central air-con Rob had obviously installed would cool it. The holes in the high-beamed ceiling, through which birds used to slip, were gone, as were the horse stalls—removed to make way for tool racks and a pneumatic lift. Partially refurbished bikes stood in neat rows, with the one Rob was currently working on—a 1975 Harley XLCH—on a table in the middle of the barn.

Rob was standing by the sink he'd installed at the far end of the building when I came in, and didn't notice me right away. When I said, "Rob," he turned around, started to say something, then noticed what I had in my arms.

Then he immediately clammed up. He leaned back against the metal sink basin, his arms folded across his chest. Dr. Phil would call this kind of body language hostile.

"I found it in Hannah's room," I said when I'd gotten close enough to him—about five feet away—that I could speak in a normal voice in the cavernous space and still be assured of being heard. "She . . . she told me about it before, but I didn't believe her."

Rob's gaze was on the album. His expression was carefully neutral. "Why wouldn't you believe her? Is it so weird I'd want to keep track of what you were doing? It's not like I could ask you. You weren't speaking to me, if you recall."

I looked down at the album, too. "Not all of this stuff is from the time when we weren't speaking."

Rob unfolded his arms and slid his fingers into the pockets of his jeans. Dr. Phil would call this a defensive gesture, too.

"All right," he said at last with a shrug. "You got me. I tried to get you out of my head—from the day I found out you were so much younger than me, I tried to get you out of my head. But I couldn't. That book's the result. I know it's creepy and weird."

I finally looked up. "I don't think it's creepy," I said. I was trying hard not to wonder if, now that I knew Hannah had been telling the truth about the scrapbook, the other things she'd said about Rob were true, too. How he kept going on to her about "how great and brave and smart and funny" I was. Did he really say those things? Did he still think they were true, now that he'd seen me again after so much time had passed?

I was also trying not to remember what had happened the last time we'd been in this barn alone together. Admittedly, it had just been some kissing . . . but Rob had always been a fantastic kisser. Not that I had so much experience to measure him by. Still, I couldn't help remembering the way my knees had always buckled at the touch of his lips to mine.

"I don't think it's weird, either," I added when he didn't say anything. "Well. Maybe a little weird. I never thought you liked me that much."

Because that, of course, was something else that had happened in this barn. I'd told him I loved him. And he had not acted too pleased about it.

Rob shrugged again. "What was I supposed to do?" he wanted to know. "You knew I was on probation. And you were underage. And the way your mom obviously felt about me—I couldn't risk it. It seemed better just to stay away from you until you turned eighteen."

"But you couldn't wait," I said. Not bitterly. I just said it like it was a fact. Because it was.

Except to Rob, apparently.

"What do you mean, I couldn't wait?" he demanded, taking his hands from his pockets and stepping away from the sink. "What do you think—Jesus, Jess! I totally waited. I'm *still* waiting."

I blinked at him. "But . . . that girl—"

"Christ. Not that again." Rob looked like he wanted

to hit something. I didn't blame him. I felt like hitting something myself. "I told you. Nancy's a customer. She *always* kisses the mechanics. She was excited about—"

"—you fixing her carburetor," I finished for him in a bored voice. Except that I wasn't bored. I was faking the bored part. The fact was, I wanted to cry. But I wouldn't let him see my tears. "You said that."

"Damned right I said that. Because it was the truth. And if you'd stuck around, instead of running off, I'd have shown you—"

He broke off. He didn't look defensive now. He looked angry. What was he so angry about?

"Shown me what?" I asked in genuine bewilderment.

"This," Rob said. He held out his arms to indicate the renovated barn, the motorcycles waiting to be serviced. "All of this. The house, the garage . . . the fact that I was going to school. Jesus, Jess. Why do you think I did all this? I mean, yeah, part of it was for me. But a big part of it was to prove to your parents—your mother, at least—that I wasn't some bum who was just after her daughter's virginity—or worse, looking to ride on your coat-tails. I did it so she'd let you go out with me. So she'd realize I'm not a worthless Grit."

Now when I blinked, it was because my eyes had filled up with tears, and I was trying to get them out of the way so I could see.

"You . . ." It was hard to talk, because something appeared to be clogging my throat. "You did all that . . . for me?"

"I was so excited when I found out you were coming back," Rob said. "Ask anyone. I knew you had lost your powers—everyone knew that. But I never thought— hell, I thought you'd be *happy* about that. No more press bugging you. No more working for the government. And you were finally eighteen . . . I thought we were golden, at last. I had this whole thing planned. I was going to show you the shop and the house and take you to that restaurant Doug was talking about today—the one in Storey—and propose. Yeah, I know it sounds ridiculous now." He added this, I guess, because he saw how my eyes widened at the word *propose*. "But that's how far gone I was. I was going to give you this—"

Digging into one of the pockets of his jeans, he pulled out a gold ring. I couldn't see it too well from where I was standing, on account of the tears. But I thought I saw a glint of diamond.

Maybe he figured out I couldn't see it. Because the next thing I knew, he'd shoved the ring roughly into my hand. Or thrown it at me, depending on how you looked at it. Good thing I've always had such excellent reflexes.

"It was my grandmother's. It's been in my family for years," Rob went on in the same half amused, half angry tone. "I know it's crazy. But I thought if your parents saw how serious I was about you, and they were okay with it, we could get married after college, or something. But instead, you showed up out of the blue, and saw something you didn't understand, and wouldn't listen to me, no matter how hard I tried to get you to. Then you just upped and left town. And I realized . . ."

"That you didn't love me after all?" I finished for him in a defensive voice. Which I actually considered pretty brave of me, considering how much I felt like running from the room, crying. The fact that I even stayed was a major step for me. Or the new, nonviolent me, anyway.

The look he gave me was almost pitying.

"No," he said in a much gentler voice. "I already told you. That you were broken. That you needed—well, nothing *I* could give you, anyway."

I laid the album down on the table next to the bike Rob had been working on. I hadn't looked at the ring.

But I hadn't let go of it, either.

"I didn't know what I needed," I said softly. "Back then."

"Do you now?" Rob asked. "Can you look me in the eye, Jess, and tell me that you finally know what you need? Or even want?"

You. Every muscle, every drop of blood in my body seemed to scream the word.

But I couldn't say it out loud. Not yet. Because what if I said it, and it wasn't what he wanted to hear? Because no one wants someone who's broken.

A beat went by. And Rob's gaze, which had been locked on mine, dropped.

"I didn't think so," he said.

And he turned back to the sink.

The conversation was over. It was *so* over.

Blinded by my tears, I still somehow made it to the door to the barn. It was only then that I turned around one last time, and said his name.

Rob didn't look back at me. But he said, "What?" to the wall in front of him.

"What did you do, anyway," I asked, "to get put on probation like that?"

His head ducked. "You want to know that *now*?"

"Yeah," I said. "I do."

"It was really stupid," he said to his hands.

"Just tell me. After all this time, I think I deserve to know."

"Trespassing," he said, still speaking to the sink. "A bunch of guys and I thought it would be funny to climb the fence to the public pool and go for a midnight swim. The officers who showed up to arrest us didn't think it was all that funny, though."

I just stared at his back. It wasn't hard not to burst

out laughing, even though he was right—it was really stupid. Stupid enough, in fact, that I realized why now he had never told me. All this time, I'd thought he'd done something . . . well, really reckless, even dangerous.

And all he'd done was go swimming when the pool was closed.

Still, I couldn't laugh. Because I was pretty sure he'd broken my heart. Again.

So instead I went back to the house and asked Chick if he would drive me home.

Which he did.

CHAPTER

18

It wasn't until I'd gotten out of Chick's truck that I realized I was still clutching the ring. Rob's grandmother's ring.

And that meant I was going to have to see him again. To give it back. Unless I took the coward's way out, and gave it to Douglas to give back to him.

Which I had pretty much decided was what I was going to do. So it was kind of funny when, just as I was putting my foot on the front step to our porch, a bright yellow Jeep pulled up into my driveway, stopping so abruptly it nearly collided with a garbage can at the curb. I recognized a very excited Tasha Thompkins sitting behind the wheel. In the passenger seat beside her sat an equally excited Douglas.

Only not for long. No sooner had Tasha put on the brakes than Douglas was bounding out of the Jeep and towards the porch steps.

"It was you, wasn't it?" Douglas demanded eagerly when he saw me. "*You* did it. You did it all!"

"Let me guess," I said, sinking down onto the porch steps. "Mr. Whitehead dropped off his check."

"Jess." Douglas's eyes were shining. Tasha, rushing up to stand beside him, didn't look any less excited. "You don't know what you've done. You don't know— you can't even imagine—how great this is."

"Well," I said mildly, "I'm kind of getting the idea. Tasha, that was the worst parking job I've ever seen."

"Finally," Douglas said, ignoring my dig at his girl-friend's driving skills, and sinking down onto the porch step beside me, "we can have a school in this town that both parents *and* kids can love. A school that doesn't suck. The kind of school you can really have pride in."

"Right," Tasha said, sitting down beside Douglas, but looking up at me. "The kind of school that someone like you might even want to come back and teach in, Jess."

I stared at them both, dumbfounded. "What? Teach? *Me?*"

"Sure," Douglas said. Then, seeing my expression, he laughed. "Well, it's not that far-fetched, Jess. Think about it. Isn't that what you're doing this summer, with Ruth?"

"Well," I said. "Yeah, but—"

"I've always thought you were great with kids, Jess,"

Tasha said. "And we're going to need a music instructor. It would be great if it could be you."

I stared at them both. "I'm not at Juilliard to train to be a music teacher," I said. "I'm there to become a professional musician."

"But is that what you want, Jess?" Tasha asked. I saw her and Douglas exchange quick glances. "To play in an orchestra? Travel around? Be a musician?"

I blinked at her. Was that what I wanted? No, actually. That wasn't what I wanted at all. What I wanted . . . what I wanted . . .

Why did everyone keep asking me what I wanted, like I was supposed to know?

"There's no need to tell us right now," Douglas said, resting a hand on my shoulder. "I mean, you'd have to wait until you've gotten your teaching certificate before you started, anyway. But if you decide you do want to come work for us, there'll always be a position for you, Jess. The pay won't be stellar, but I promise it will be enough to live on. And for gas, for Blue Beauty."

He grinned at me. I couldn't help grinning back. His excitement was catching.

It's ironic that Mom should have chosen that moment to pull up herself.

"Oh," Tasha said, standing up and looking worried. "I've blocked the driveway."

But Mom was already parking on the street. She didn't even appear to notice Tasha or her Jeep. She didn't even notice Douglas. All of her attention was focused on me.

Which was so not what I needed just then.

"Jessica," she said, even as she was still climbing out of her car. "Just what exactly *was* that this morning? You swept out of here without a word of apology to poor Karen Sue. I understand you had other things to do than have brunch with her—believe me, it's all over town, what you were up to this morning. But couldn't you have at least said you were sorry and rescheduled for another time?"

"Mom," Douglas said, standing up. "You are never going to believe what Jess did. She—"

"I already heard all about what your sister did," Mom said. She'd crossed the street into our yard now and noticed the garbage can Tasha had nearly hit. She started tugging it towards the garage. "That's just lovely, Jessica, getting yourself involved in busting up a porn ring. I understand that Wilkins boy was there, as well. Why am I not surprised?"

"Mom." Douglas looked annoyed. "Jessica got Mr. Whitehead to donate three million dollars to—"

"I beg your pardon, Douglas," Mom said, glaring at him. "But I am speaking to Jessica. Well?" She brushed her hands off on her slacks. "What do you have to say for yourself? Because I had to stand here and try to keep Karen Sue from crying—yes, *crying*—over how you treated her this morning. I understand that perhaps you had more pressing concerns, but . . ." Her eyes narrowed behind her sunglasses as she stared at the porch. "What's going on with you, Jessica? You look . . . different."

Maybe because right then, I was thinking about killing her.

"Ma," Douglas said. "She—"

"Don't call me Ma," Mom said automatically. "Jessica, what exactly is going on here? You show up out of the blue, and the next thing I know, you're involved in some kind of teen runaway porn scandal. You should have seen Mrs. Leskowski's expression when she came up to me in the Kroger just now to tell me all about it. Butter wouldn't have melted in that woman's mouth. It's almost like she thinks the rest of us don't remember what Mark did—"

Suddenly Mom whipped off her sunglasses, apparently to get a better look at me. *"Jessica. Did you get your powers back?"*

Oh, brother.

"I gotta go," I said, getting up. Because suddenly, I had a burning need to take my bike out for a little spin.

"Wait," Mom said. "Jessica. Did you? You did, didn't you? Oh, Jessica."

"Come on, Mom." Douglas looked annoyed. "Get with the program. You want to know the *really* good news? She got Randy Whitehead to donate three million—"

"Why didn't you tell me, Jessica?" Mom, ignoring Douglas, asked me. "Does Dr. Krantz know?"

My eyes widened. "God. I hope not."

"Well, Jessica. You have to tell him. I mean, there are still people out there that I'm sure they'd like to—"

"Mom!" I stared at her. I couldn't believe this. I really couldn't. I was so distracted that I found myself slipping Rob's grandmother's ring on and off my left middle finger. Then I figured I'd better leave it on, so I wouldn't lose it. I had to give it back to him, after all.

"You can't have it both ways," I said, coming down off the porch steps and heading for Blue Beauty. "You can't have a daughter who's normal, like Karen Sue Hankey, and a daughter with psychic powers, like me. You have to decide. You have to decide which one you want."

Because that's what my Juilliard scholarship, I knew, represented to my mom—that I was normal. Which is what she'd always wanted—a normal daughter, like Karen Sue Hankey. Not one who wouldn't put on a dress, loved motorcycles, and could find missing people in her sleep.

Well, she'd gotten her wish. For the entirety of this past year, I'd been the normal daughter Mom had always wanted.

But no more. No more normal for me.

Was she going to be able to deal with that?

Was *I*?

"Jessica," Mom said, stepping in front of me, effectively blocking my path to the garage. "I have no idea what you're talking about."

"Just that maybe if you had ever supported me in anything I ever did—besides going to Juilliard—I might have turned out more the way you wanted me to."

Mom's eyebrows went up. WAY up.

"What are you talking about?" she demanded. "You know your father and I have always supported you, in everything you've ever done—"

"Not about Rob, you didn't," I said.

Mom looked shocked. "Is *that* what this is about? That boy? I can't believe you're even giving him a second's thought, after the way he treated you—"

"He treated me that way because of *you*, Mom. Because of your stupid statutory-rape speech. You totally scared him off—"

"I'm glad I did," Mom said indignantly. "Jessica, I know you've always had self-esteem issues, but believe me, you can do a lot better than a common grease monkey with a criminal record."

"For swimming after hours at a public pool, Ma," I said. "That's what Rob was on probation for. For trespassing."

Behind me, I heard Douglas burst out laughing. "For real?" he wanted to know. "That's why he got busted?"

I whirled around to face him. "It's not funny!" I shrieked. Although, of course, ordinarily I probably would have found it hilarious. All that wondering, all that worrying, for years, and over what? A midnight swim.

I swung back around to face Mom. But before I could get a word out, she was saying, "If he really loved you, Jessica, he'd have waited for you. The fact that he did run away, just because of my little speech . . . well, that shows you something about him, doesn't it?"

"Yes," I said tensely. "It shows me that he loved me enough to respect my parents' wishes. And do you have any idea what he did while he was waiting for me to turn eighteen, Ma?"

"I've told you before," she said irritably. "Don't call me Ma."

"He bought his own business," I went on as if she hadn't spoken. "And his own house. He's probably earning *more* than a hundred thousand a year, fixing up motorcycles for rich Baby Boomers, *and* he's going to college at the same time. What do you think about *that*, Ma?"

"I think," Mom said, her mouth flattening to a straight line, "that you're forgetting one very important thing."

"*What?*"

"That you saw him kissing another girl. You've never seen Skip kissing another girl, have you?"

I stepped around her and headed to my bike.

"Well?" Mom wanted to know. "Have you? No. You haven't, have you?"

"Only because no other girl would *let* Skip kiss her," Douglas pointed out, causing Tasha to start laughing so hard, she had to slap a hand over her mouth to stifle it.

I pulled my bike from the garage, kicking the doors closed behind me with one booted foot.

"Where are you going?" Mom demanded. "Wait, don't tell me. You're going to see *him*, aren't you?"

"No," I said, lowering my helmet over my head. "I'm going to get away from *you*."

And then I gunned my engine a few more times than was strictly necessary, just to drown out whatever Mom said next, and drove away.

CHAPTER

19

"Ruth?"

The voice on the other end of the phone sounded groggy. "Jess? Is that you? God, what time is it?"

I glanced at the alarm clock on my nightstand. "Oops," I said. "It's one in the morning. Sorry, I didn't realize it was so late. Did I wake you up?"

"Yeah, you woke me up." Now Ruth sounded less groggy and more alarmed. "What's wrong?"

"Nothing's wrong," I said. I held the cell phone closer to my ear, blinking up at the ceiling in my night-darkened bedroom. After an evening of driving aimlessly around the countryside—then returning home to find Mom still sulking in her room, and Dad working late at the restaurant—I'd amused myself by watching home-improvement shows.

Only all these did was make me think of Rob, who'd done a much better job improving his house than any of the people I saw on TV.

"I mean, nothing's really wrong," I said to Ruth. "I just . . . I really need to talk to you. I think . . . I think I did something really stupid."

"What did you do?" Ruth asked, her voice filled with dread.

"I . . . I think Rob proposed, and I just sort of . . . walked out."

"You think Rob proposed?" I could tell Ruth was sitting up, since her voice suddenly got much clearer. "What do you mean, you *think* he proposed? Did he give you a ring?"

I gazed at Rob's grandmother's ring, still around the third finger on my left hand. It was dark in my room, but I could still make out the diamond in the middle of the band. There were smaller diamonds set all around it, in some curlicue gold stuff. I bet Karen Sue Hankey would know what that curlicue gold stuff was called.

"Well," I said. "Yes. But—"

"Holy crap," Ruth said. "He *proposed*!"

Which is when a male voice, sounding like it was coming from somewhere very close to Ruth, said in the background, "He *what*?"

The weird thing was, I could have sworn the voice was Mikey's.

"Ruth?" I asked in the silence that followed. "Was that—"

"That was Skip," Ruth said quickly. "He came in here to see who I was talking to."

"Really," I said. "Because it sounded like he was in bed with you. And it sounded more like—"

"I can't believe Rob proposed!" Ruth interrupted. "That is amazing, Jess! I mean, isn't it?"

"Yeah, but that's the thing. He didn't *really* propose. He told me he was *going* to propose when I got back from Afghanistan. But then I—well, you know."

"Saw him with Miss Boobs-As-Big-As-Your-Head?"

"Right. And he seemed to think it would be better if he just let me go through whatever it was he seemed to think I was going through, at the time."

"Which," Ruth said, "in retrospect, wasn't such a bad thing, Jess. I mean, you have to admit, you were a mess back then."

This was so not what I called her to hear.

"What happened to *'he's the guy who let you walk away when you needed him most'*?" I asked indignantly. "Suddenly you're on his side?"

"Of course not," Ruth said. "But look how things turned out. You're a lot better now. And he still gave you the ring. Which means he must still want to. Marry you, I mean."

"I'm not sure," I said. "He didn't so much as give me the ring as throw it at me. And I just sort of hung on to it. The thing is, Ruth—" And suddenly I found myself pouring out the whole story—Hannah, and Randy, and the videotapes, and the scrapbook, and the things Rob had told me that afternoon. All of it.

And when I'd finished, Ruth said, "Well, it's obvious he's still in love with you. The question is, are you still in love with him? I mean, would you take him back? In spite of Miss Boobs-As-Big-As-Your-Head?"

I had to think about that.

"It's not like she's in the picture anymore," I said slowly. "I mean, that I can see. And, I mean, we were broken up then . . . sort of. The thing is, I don't even know if he'd take me back. You know, if I offered."

"He gave you a ring."

"He THREW it at me."

"Well, why don't you ask him?"

"What? Just go up to him and be all, *'Hey, do you still want to marry me?'*"

"Basically, yeah. Why not?"

I stared at the ceiling. "Because what if he says no? What if he thinks I'm still"—I swallowed—"broken?"

"Then you give him the ring back, say sayonara, and hop on the first flight back here, and I'll find you a totally hot new guy who fully appreciates what an amazing person you are."

"Tell her if she wants us to, we'll still beat him up for her," whispered the male voice very close to Ruth, apparently thinking I wouldn't overhear.

Only I did.

And this time, I knew it wasn't Skip.

"Ruth," I said. "Why is my brother Mike in BED WITH YOU?"

"Crap," Ruth said. Then, apparently to Mike, she said, "I told you she could hear you."

"Hi, Jess," Mikey called in the background.

"Oh my God." I was sitting up, convinced I was going to hyperventilate. It wasn't as if I hadn't seen it coming. It was just so . . . so . . .

Gross.

"I can't believe I only go away for two days," I said disgustedly, "and you two have already hopped into bed together."

"Jess," Ruth said, sounding worried. "It's not like that, really. I—I—"

"Oh my God," I said. "If you say you love my brother, I'll barf. I swear it."

"Well, it's true," Ruth said. "I think I always have—"

While this was true, I still didn't want to have to hear about it.

"Put Mike on the phone," I said to her.

"But, Jess—"

"Just do it."

A second later, Mike's deep voice was saying, "Jess. It's not what you think. I really—"

"If you break her heart," I said to him, "I will break your face. Do you understand?"

Mike sounded stunned. "Isn't that what you said to Tasha, about Douglas?"

"Yes."

"Shouldn't you be saying that to Ruth, and not me?"

"No," I said. "Because in this instance, my loyalties lie with Ruth, not you."

"Oh, thanks a lot," Mike said, sounding sarcastic.

"Well," I said. "She's my best friend. You're just my brother."

"I happen," Mike said, "to love her."

"Oh God." The nachos I'd heated up in the microwave for dinner came up a little. "You're going to make me sick. Literally. Put Ruth back on the phone."

"Did Rob really propose?"

"Put Ruth back on the phone."

"What are you going to say? Yes? If you say yes, are you going to stay in Indiana?"

"Why?" I asked, though I wasn't sure I wanted to know.

"Because if you stay in Indiana, then I can move in

here with Ruth," he said, "when I transfer to Columbia."

"You're transferring schools for a girl? *Again?* Did you forget what happened last time you did that?"

"Shut up, Jess," Mike said. "It's different this time."

"You better believe it is," I said. "Because if you screw this one up, you're—"

"—dead. Yes, I got the picture, thanks. So. What are you going to do?"

"If one more person asks me that," I began in a warning tone. Then I broke off, struck by a thought. "Hey, where's Skip, anyway? What does he think about how you guys have turned the place into a den of sin? What does he think about what you're doing to his *sister*?"

"Skip's at the Jersey Shore," Mike said. "With some girl he—"

"Okay, that's enough about Skip," Ruth said, apparently having wrestled the phone back from my brother. "When are you coming home? *Are* you coming home?"

"I don't know," I said, chewing my lower lip. I hadn't mentioned anything to her about Douglas's offer of a teaching job at his new alternative high school. Because I wasn't sure I could stay in this town, knowing that Rob was living in it, too, and not be with him.

As if she were the one with the psychic powers, and

not me, Ruth said, "Jess. Just ask him. Okay? Now get some sleep."

She hung up.

I sat there, blinking down at my cell phone. Then I placed it gently on the nightstand and flopped back down against the pillows. How was it, I wondered, that everyone—everyone I knew, anyway—was getting some, except for me? What had I done wrong? How had I screwed everything up in that arena so very, very badly?

It was kind of ironic that as I was thinking this to myself, a hailstorm of rocks suddenly struck the bay windows in my bedroom. Not hard enough to break the glass, but definitely hard enough for the loud rattle they made to wake me . . .

. . . if I'd actually been asleep, that is.

Only one person had ever thrown pebbles at my bedroom window before. The same person who, earlier that day, had thrown an engagement ring at me.

Tossing back my comforter, I went to the closest window and peered down, hardly daring to hope that it would actually be him.

But it was. He was standing in the moonlight in jeans and a black T-shirt, just pulling his arm back to let loose another volley of stones. I hastily flung open the window and screen, leaned out, and whispered, "Hold on. I'll be right down."

Then I grabbed a cotton robe I'd thrown into my overnight bag when I'd packed so hastily for the trip home, and slipped it on over my tank top and boxers. I wished I, like Ruth, had given a little more thought to my nightwear, and maybe bought something a little sexier to wear to bed, like her cute camis and matching tap pants, which my brother Mike was apparently currently—ew, that was WAY too gross to think about.

Besides, Rob wasn't here, I'm sure, because of any romantic feelings he might be harboring for me. Probably his sister had run away again.

Or maybe he just wanted his ring back.

The thought caused me to pause midway down the stairs.

That's right. He probably wanted his ring back.

And suddenly, I found I couldn't breathe.

My heart banging ridiculously hard in my ears, I crept the rest of the way down the stairs. The house was in darkness. Both my parents were asleep. Only Chigger was awake. He climbed down off the living room couch—the one Mom had forbidden him from sleeping on, so he only did it when she wasn't looking—and came to the door to greet me.

"Sit," I said to him, quietly unlocking the front door. "Stay."

The dog did neither. He licked my hand, then walked silently back to the sofa and climbed back onto it. So much for knowing over fifteen commands.

I opened the screen door and slipped out onto the porch. Rob was already there waiting in the shadow from the porch roof cast by the moonlight. I couldn't see his eyes. They just looked like twin pools of darkness to me.

But I could see the place in his neck where his pulse beat. For some reason, a shaft of moonlight fell right across it.

And I could see it was thrumming almost as fast as my own.

"Hey," he said in a soft voice.

It was a neutral *hey*. Sort of a questioning *hey*. Not like *Hey, good to see you*. More like, *Hey . . . what's going on here?*

Like I knew.

"They have this new invention now," I whispered. "It's called cell phones. You can call people now in the middle of the night, if you need to, instead of throwing rocks at their window."

Rob said, "You never gave me your cell number."

"Oh." Well, I never said I wasn't an idiot.

And suddenly, I knew. I knew why he was there. And it had nothing to do with his sister.

Cold hard fear gripped my heart. I found myself slipping my left hand behind my back.

Because I knew then. I knew I wasn't giving that ring back. Not unless he pried it off my dead body. I'd never worn a ring before in my life—I'm not exactly a jewelry girl.

But I'd gotten used to wearing this one, and fast. I wasn't ready to give it up. I didn't *want* to give it up.

And I knew, right there on the porch, that I wasn't going to. Instead, I was going to do what Ruth had told me to.

I was going to ask him.

Unless, of course, I didn't have to. Because if he held out his hand and went, "Give it back," that would be a pretty strong indicator that the answer was no.

"Are you missing something?" I asked him, still keeping my hand behind my back. "Something else, besides your sister, I mean? Is that why you're here?"

A strange sort of expression passed across his face. I couldn't tell what it was, exactly, because his head was still in shadow. But I saw some of the tension seem to leave his shoulders.

"My sister left this afternoon," he said. "With her mother. After stopping off at the police station for about a trillion hours. Hannah's not what I'm missing."

I held up my left hand.

"Is it this, then?"

He sucked in his breath.

"You have it?" he asked. "God, I thought I was going crazy. I was looking everywhere."

"You couldn't wait until morning?" I asked him. "You had to come get it now, in the middle of the night?"

"I didn't realize you must have taken it," he said, "until a little while ago. And then I—"

He broke off. I still couldn't see his face so well. But it was clear he wasn't exactly smiling.

"You what?" I asked.

"I had to know," he said, finally, with a shrug, "if you took it. Well, not so much *if*. More like . . . *why*."

My heart still banging in my ears, I took a step towards him. I knew the moonlight was full on my face. But I didn't care. I didn't care what he saw there.

"Why do you think?" I asked, tilting my chin up.

"I don't know what to think," Rob said. "The whole way here, I was thinking I was crazy. I mean, why *would* you take it? Unless . . ."

He took a step towards me. I still held up my left hand. The moonlight caught on the diamond, and caused it to sparkle crazily.

"Jess," Rob said in a cautious voice. "What are you doing? Seriously."

"Seriously?" I shook my head. "I really don't know." Because I really didn't. All I knew was that my throat was dry as sand and that my heart was doing crazy things inside my chest. I think it might have been a jig. "But you're like the hundredth person to ask me that today. Do you want it back?"

"If you're not gonna marry me," Rob said. He seemed confused. I didn't blame him. "Then, yeah, I want it back."

"What if I am?" I asked him, though it was kind of hard to talk, considering the fact that I couldn't seem to breathe anymore.

"Am what?"

Then Rob took a step forward that brought him out from beneath the shadow of the porch roof. And even though his back was still to the moon, I could see his eyes.

"Jess," he said in a warning tone.

Which is when I took the deepest breath I could—considering I couldn't seem to inhale at all—reached out to grab a fistful of his shirt, dragged him the two-step space between us, and said, my face just a few inches below his, "Rob. Will you marry me?"

He looked down at me expressionlessly. "You," he said, "are insane."

"I mean it," I said. Amazingly, the second the words

were out of my mouth, the crazy banging in my ears stopped. And I could breathe. I could actually breathe. "I've been an idiot. I had a lot of crap to deal with. And I think I'm done dealing with it now. Almost all of it, anyway. Obviously I still have to finish school—and so do you—and all of that. But when we're done with school, I think we should do it."

Rob looked about as serious as I'd ever seen him look. "What about your mom?" he asked.

"In case you haven't noticed, I'm over eighteen," I pointed out. "Besides, she'll come around. So, are you in?"

I will admit, it wasn't exactly easy to breathe while I was waiting for his reply. In fact, it was impossible.

So it was a good thing he said, "I'm in," before I ran out of oxygen and collapsed right there onto the porch.

I grinned up at him. "Good," I said.

And then, just like that, we were kissing.

Well, okay, maybe not just like that. I might have had something to do with it, by standing up on my tip-toes and throwing my arms around his neck.

I am definitely responsible for what happened next, which was that I grabbed another handful of his shirt and started leading him to the front door.

"Jess." Rob was grinning. Even in the shadow of the porch roof, I could see his smile. "What are you doing?"

"Shhhh," I said. "Follow me. And be quiet or you'll wake them."

"Jess." Rob let himself be led inside as far as the foyer before he put on the brakes. "Come on," he whispered, as Chigger came over from the couch to give him a few desultory licks before retiring again. "This isn't right."

"No one'll ever know," I assured him. "You can sneak out before they wake up. Besides," I added, "it's all right. *We're engaged.*"

Which is how Rob got to see my room that night for the first time. And a lot more than just my room, actually.

CHAPTER
20

He woke up before I did.

"Jess," he was whispering, when I opened my eyes to find the gray light of dawn turning my bedroom walls pink. Also to find Rob putting his shirt back on, a sight truly worth waking up so early for. "I'm gonna go."

"Don't," I said, throwing my arms around his waist. I'd apparently missed the putting back on of the jeans. Too bad.

"I have to," he said, laughingly prying my arms off him. "What if your parents wake up? Is that really how you want them finding out about us?"

Flopping disgruntledly back against the pillows, I said, "I guess not. Still. What are you doing later?"

"Seeing you," Rob said as he sat down on my window seat to tug on his motorcycle boots. It was extremely odd to see Rob Wilkins in my bedroom at all.

But it was especially weird to see him sitting on the

lace-covered pillows with which my mom had decorated the built-in window seat beneath my bay windows. It was sort of like seeing Batman shopping for shampoo at the drugstore, or something. Just completely out of place.

"I have to go to the garage for a while," Rob said after he'd gotten both shoes on, and stood up. "Want to come over and grab some lunch around noon?"

"I could bring you lunch," I said. "I could make some sandwiches and cupcakes or something."

Rob looked at me. "Did you just say you'd make cupcakes?"

"Yeah," I said apologetically. "I don't know what came over me. Since that would so never happen."

"I'm sure if you did make cupcakes someday," Rob said chivalrously, "they'd be delicious."

"No, they wouldn't."

"Well, no, you're probably right. Still. It was a nice thought."

"I'll just see you at noon," I said. And rolled out of bed. "Here, let me walk you out."

Rob tried to argue with me, that he could find his own way downstairs. But I didn't want to run the risk of him running into one of my parents alone. I didn't want him calling off the engagement after only six hours.

But I managed to get him out of the house safely.

The only person in the house besides us who was up was Chigger, and he just checked us for food. Not finding any, he went back to the couch.

I stood on the porch in the cool morning air. Even though it was so early, I wasn't a bit tired. That's because I'd slept like a log for a change.

"Where's your truck?" I asked when I'd looked around and seen only a nondescript sedan and—hilariously—a Trans Am parked on the street.

"I parked around the corner," Rob admitted with a sheepish smile, before kissing me good-bye. "I didn't want to arouse the suspicions of your neighbors."

"You're such a gentleman," I said. He'd started down the porch steps, but I held on to one of his hands. "Hey, Rob?"

"What?"

"Did my dad buy my bike from you? Blue Beauty, I mean?"

Rob's grin was crooked. "Yeah. He asked me what kind of bike I thought you'd like, and . . . well, I had that one picked out for you a long time before he asked. Let's put it that way."

"I knew it," I said, my heart feeling as if it were about to bubble over with joy. "Bye."

"Bye."

He seemed to be having trouble containing the

bubbling over of his own heart—at least if the way he smiled at me was any indication. I had never seen him look so happy.

Then he left, hurrying down the street to get his truck. I stood and watched him disappear around the corner. In fact, that's why I didn't notice the driver's door to the Trans Am parked across the street had opened. Because I was too busy watching Rob disappear around the corner.

Which is why I didn't realize Randy Whitehead Junior was coming towards me until he was halfway across the yard.

"Randy," I said when I finally noticed him. "When'd you make bail?"

Seriously it didn't even occur to me to be scared. That's how giddy I still was from everything that had happened during the night.

Even when Randy didn't say anything—just kept coming towards me with a very intent expression on that weaselly looking face, hovering beneath his hundred-dollar haircut—it didn't seem weird. I just assumed he hadn't heard me.

"What are you doing here, Randy?" I asked him. "You come to apologize?"

But when he climbed the steps up to where I was standing in two long strides, then seized me by the throat with one hand, throwing me back against the screen door, I realized he hadn't actually come over to apologize.

"You," he pressed his cheek against mine to whisper into my ear, "have ruined my life."

I tried to scream. I really did. But his hand was crushing my larynx. I couldn't even breathe, let alone utter a sound.

I would like to add that Randy smelled extremely ripe, a combination of body odor, Calvin For Men, and what I was pretty sure was tequila. My eyes started to water, and not just from lack of oxygen, either.

"I wasn't hurting anybody," he hissed raggedly in my ear. "Those girls wanted it. They *wanted* it. And now my mom says I'm a disgrace, and my dad says—you know what my dad says?"

I was clawing at his hands, trying to get them off my neck. I'd tried kicking him, but being barefoot, I didn't seem to be doing much damage. I tried kneeing him in the groin, but he kept moving out of the way. It was hard to get much leverage, anyway, considering the fact that he was holding me a couple of inches off the ground.

"My dad says if I kill you, to keep you from telling my mom about Eric, he might even forgive me for being such a screwup someday." Randy's breath was as ripe as the rest of him. It had been a while since he'd hit the mints. "So that's why I'm here. I was hoping you'd come out of the house and get on that bike of yours, and I could just wait till no one else was around, and knock you off it and into a ditch or something. But you know what? I like this better. Because, take a look – no one else is around. Just you. And me."

It was hard to tell, over the roaring in my ears. But I thought I could hear Chigger barking. Yes. Chigger was definitely barking. And hurling himself angrily against the screen door, right behind. I could feel his claws. That ought to wake Mom and Dad up. *Good boy, Chigger. Good boy.*

"I'll tell you what, though," Randy said. "I'll let you go if you tell *me* who Eric is. Because I really, really want to know."

And he loosened his hold on my throat—just a little—so that I could tell him. I choked down a lungful of air. And croaked, "Bite me."

Wham! The hands went right back around my neck.

"That's not very polite," Randy commented. "Jesus, why won't that dog shut the hell *up?*"

On the word *up*, something happened to Randy's head. It disappeared.

Or at least, that's how it seemed from my angle. It wasn't until his hands suddenly left my throat again—

and I was falling to the porch floor, gasping for breath—that I realized Randy's head was still very much attached to Randy's body. It had just seemed to disappear, due to the force of the blow Rob had delivered to his jaw.

Collapsed against the screen door, I was in the perfect position to watch Rob pummel the life out of Randy Whitehead Junior. I got to see some bloody bits of capped tooth fly by—very gratifying—and was able to explain to my startled parents, who'd finally been roused from bed, that the reason Rob was killing Randy Whitehead was that Randy had been trying to kill me.

Still, it wasn't my dad who broke up the fight—though, to his credit, he tried, which was an almost comical sight, this middle-aged man in boxers and an undershirt, trying to pull Rob off the drunk pornographer who'd taken advantage of his sister, and then tried to kill his fiancée.

No, it was the man who strode into my yard right after that, gun drawn, and shouted, "All of you! Freeze, or I'll shoot! FBI!"

"Oh," my mother said from where she'd been helping me up from the porch floor. "Good morning, Dr. Krantz."

Keeping his pistol trained on Randy—who really didn't look as if he was too eager to go anywhere, anyway—Cyrus Krantz said, "Good morning, Toni. I was hoping I wasn't too early to stop by for coffee. I can see now that I came just in time. Up to your old tricks again, eh, Jessica?"

By that time, my dad had managed to pry Rob off Randy. Now Rob reached up to dab at his bloody lower lip with the back of a hand, before glancing at me and saying with a grin, "I told you it was time you let someone rescue *you* for a change."

"Good one," I croaked. It hurt to talk. "What brought you back here?"

He held up a bare wrist. "I forgot my watch."

"Aw," I said. "Of course. It's on my nightstand."

"What," my mom wanted to know, "is going on here? Jessica, why was this man trying to kill you? And why is Rob here? And what's his watch doing on your nightstand?"

"Oh," I said, holding up my left hand to show her Rob's grandmother's ring. "It's all right. We're engaged."

"Mazel tov," said Dr. Krantz. He hadn't stopped pointing his gun at Randy Whitehead Junior, who was still moaning on the porch floor.

"You're *what*?" Mom yelled. Then, to my dad, she shrieked, "Will you shut that dog of yours up?"

"Chigger! Down," Dad yelled. And the dog stopped barking. "Toni. I think you should go inside and call the police."

"Already done," Dr. Krantz said, hanging up his cell phone. "I asked for an ambulance, too. That young man's nose appears to be broken."

My mom stayed where she was. "You're *engaged*?" she asked me, looking astonished.

"Oh, yeah," Rob said, running a hand through his dark hair and making it stand up even more wildly on end. "This probably isn't a good time to ask, but Mr. and Mrs. Mastriani, I'd like to marry your daughter, if that's all right with you. Well, I'm going to even if it isn't all right. But I'd prefer to have your blessing."

"She has to finish college first," my dad said with a grunt, from where he was examining the bloodstains on the porch floor. "I'm gonna need to hit those with the hose before they dry or they'll never come out."

"Joe!" My mother's eyes were filled with tears. "Is that all you have to say about this?"

"Well, whadduya want me to say?" Dad asked. "He's a good guy. Look what he just did. He saved our daughter's life."

"Yeah," I said to her hoarsely. "Skip never did that."

"I need coffee," Mom whimpered, just as the wail of a police siren filled the air.

"Mom." It was hard to talk, since my throat still hurt pretty badly. But I put my arm around her and gave her a squeeze. "Don't think of it as losing a daughter. Think of it as finally getting her back."

My mom looked down at me. She tried to smile, though the result was a bit watery.

"I don't understand a single thing that's happening right now," she said. "But . . ." She looked over at Rob, who was carefully watching her. "Welcome to the family, Rob."

A relieved grin broke out over Rob's face. "Thanks, Mrs. Mastriani," he said.

"Oh, what the heck," Mom said, as the first of the police cruisers came screaming up in front of the house. "Call me Ma."

CHAPTER
21

It wasn't until the ambulance had taken Randy away—
in police custody, for the second time in twenty-four
hours—and I'd given my statement (this time they let
me write it in my own dining room. I didn't have to go
down to the station house, for a change), and Rob and
my dad had gone off to work, and my mom had retired
to her bedroom with a migraine, that I finally got to
shower and dress, then sit down with the man who had,
after all, come all the way from Washington, DC, to
see me.

It was weird to find him sitting on my porch swing.
Weird, and yet strangely not weird, too. There'd been a
time when the sight of him had terrified me, because
he'd represented everything I didn't want—the glare of
the media spotlight that had, once upon a time, so upset
Douglas; working for a government I didn't trust, with
an agency I wasn't sure I believed in.

Then I'd gotten to know him—Cyrus—better and realized he actually really did mean well. And that the truth is, he's just a huge nerd with a secret liking for peanut M&M's. He was even dressed in the height of nerd summer chic, in a short-sleeved dress shirt with a clip-on tie, khakis, and pocket protector, which is what he'd worn almost daily in Afghanistan, as well. The only difference was that here in the U.S., he preferred an ankle holster for his service piece. Over there, it had been a shoulder holster.

It was nice to know some things, anyway, never changed.

"So what are you doing here?" I asked him—not in an unfriendly way. "Oh, no, wait. Let me guess: You heard I got my powers back."

"Kind of hard to keep something like that a secret," Cyrus said, reaching for the cup of coffee my mom had poured for him—and all the officers—before retiring. "Especially when you're using it to bust up interstate amateur porn rings."

I just looked at him. "You tapped my cell phone, didn't you?"

"Of course," he said. "When you called all of those girls yesterday morning to tell them what Randy had done and how you intended to punish him . . . that was inspired. And you called their parents, as well, to see if they'd welcome their daughters home, but carefully didn't reveal to them just where, exactly, their child was . . . that was brilliant, as well. Some of your best work, I would have to say."

"I wish," I said, "that you guys would cut it out. The phone tapping stuff, I mean. Because I'm not coming back, you know."

"To work for us," Cyrus asked, "or New York?"

"Neither," I said. "I mean . . . both."

"Jessica," Cyrus said, shaking his head. "I wouldn't dream of asking."

I blinked at him. "Really? That's not why you're here?"

"Certainly not. You know, we've all been so worried about you. It's good to hear you're feeling better. And I'm especially pleased to hear about you and Rob. That's some excellent news. And I understand your brother's asked you to come teach at this alternative school he's opening. Are you going to do that?"

"Yes," I said guardedly. I couldn't believe it. He wasn't going to ask me to come back? *Really?* "I'm going to transfer to Indiana and get my teaching certificate."

"Very good. You were always excellent with children. What I really came here to say, Jessica, since you ask, is that . . . well, I know we've had our differences in the past. But I think all we've both ever wanted is to help make this world a better place. God knows, you've done more than your share in this capacity. We pushed you . . . well, we pushed you more than we should have, and the result was that eventually, you had nothing left to give. Now that you've got your powers back, what you do with them is entirely your own choice. No one would fault you if you decided never to use them again. You have many other strengths, and I fully expect that you'll have just as much success bettering the planet using them as you did using your psychic abilities. But, in the off chance you should like to come back—"

"Aha!" I cried. Then wished I hadn't because the word really strained my already swollen throat.

Still, I'd known this was coming. And not because I have ESP, either.

"—I wanted to let you know there will always be a place for you on my team."

Wait. What?

I stared at him some more. "That's it? No begging?"

"No begging."

"No guilt trips?"

"None of those, either. You've done your duty, Jessica. No one—least of all me—could ask you to do anymore. If you wanted to, that's another story. But since you don't . . ." He shrugged, as if to say, *So be it.*

"You're serious?" I still couldn't quite believe it. "I'm off the hook?"

"Completely."

"No more tapping my phone?"

"None."

"No more following me?"

"None."

"You're not going to call a press conference to announce my return to the world of psychic people-finding?"

"Not unless you wish me to."

"Or tell me about some kid missing in Des Moines whose Mommy wants him back so dearly?"

"Jessica." Cyrus Krantz climbed to his feet. "I already told you. You have done more than your fair share of good for others in this world. I think it's time you concentrated on doing some good for yourself for a change. And that's what I came here to tell you."

I had to crane my neck to see his face, since he was towering so far above me.

"It is not," I said. "You came here to see if I wanted to come back."

"Well," he admitted, looking sheepish. "Of course. But since you don't want to, well, that's another story. So instead I'll just wish you luck. Call me if you ever need anything. And tell your mother I hope she'll be feeling better soon. I'm sure she will. The thing with you and Rob . . . well, it will just take some getting used to for her. But she's a sensible woman. She'll come around."

"I know she will," I said.

He hesitated on the top step. "Of course, if something came along that we *really* needed your help on . . ."

Now *this* was more like the Cyrus I knew.

"You can call me," I said with a laugh.

He looked visibly relieved.

"Good," he said. "Well, that's all I wanted to know. Good-bye for now. And remember . . . it's time to do some good for *you*, Jessica."

With that proclamation, he strolled back to the waiting four-door sedan with the tinted windows—not the same one that had been parked in front of my house yesterday morning—that I hadn't noticed until just then, the one that had been parked just a little down the street from Randy's Trans Am.

No sooner had he driven away than my cell phone chirped. I pulled it from my back pocket and said, "Hello?"

All I could hear on the other end was shrieking.

"Yes, Ruth," I said calmly. "How'd you find out?"

"Mike just got off the phone with your dad," Ruth said. "Can I be a bridesmaid?"

"Ew," I said. "No way. I'm not having any of those."

"What?" Ruth sounded majorly disappointed. "Why not?"

"Um, because it's my wedding, and I'm not having any bridesmaids," I pointed out. "You can be my witness, if you want."

"Do I get to wear a cute dress?"

"You can wear whatever you want. I don't care."

"Your mom," Ruth said, "is going to be so disappointed in this whole affair, I can just tell. But I'm really happy for you."

"Yeah," I said sarcastically. "Because now you get to share your room with Mike and not me."

"Shut up," Ruth said, laughing. "You were an awesome roommate. Well, except for the night terrors. Speaking of terror, how's your mom coping with it, anyway?"

"She'll be all right," I said. Because I knew she would be. Eventually.

"Does Douglas know?"

"Not yet. Rob and I are meeting him and Tasha for lunch in—" I looked at the time. "Right now, actually. I have to go. I'll talk to you later. And, Ruth?"

"Yeah?"

"Can I be *your* bridesmaid? When you marry Mike?"

Ruth, as I'd known she would, screamed happily

again and hung up. Smiling, I went to the garage and pulled out my bike, then cruised on over to Wilkins Auto and Motorcycle Repair. I can't say that, when I pulled up to the light on First and Main, and noticed Karen Sue Hankey in the white convertible in the lane next to me, I was particularly surprised. I raised the face shield of my helmet and yelled, "Karen Sue!"

She looked over at me, startled. "Jess?"

"Hey," I said. "Sorry about blowing you off yesterday. I had a lot on my mind."

"I know," Karen Sue said unsmilingly. "I read the paper this morning."

"So," I said. "Want to reschedule?"

"Sure," Karen Sue said. "When are you leaving to go back to New York?"

"Oh," I said. "Never."

Karen Sue's mouth fell open. "What?"

"I'm staying here," I said with a shrug.

"Here?" Karen Sue looked shocked. *"Why?"*

"Because," I said. The light turned green. "I'm engaged to a local business owner. Call me!"

I left Karen Sue sitting at the light in shock. When I glanced in my rearview mirror before making the turn into the parking lot of Rob's garage, I saw that she was still sitting there, openmouthed, a line of cars behind her, honking.

Rob had done a lot, I saw at a glance, to his uncle's garage. For one thing, the place was a lot cleaner. And for another, they were servicing European cars as well as American and Japanese models. In fact, as I walked up, I saw Rob in gray coveralls, bent over the engine of a butter-colored Mercedes coupe, behind the wheel of which sat a woman with a lot of blond hair who looked a little familiar, though I couldn't place her face. At first.

"Try it again," Rob said to the blonde, who obediently switched on her ignition.

The motor purred to life. Rob, looking satisfied, put the hood down.

"It was just your starter again," he said, reaching for a rag to wipe the grease from his hands. "It shouldn't give you any more trouble. Just—"

But he didn't get to finish, because the blonde had leaped out of the car and hurled herself against him, throwing both arms around his neck.

"Oh, Rob! You are such a miracle worker!" she cried. "I can't thank you enough!"

And then she laid a great, big kiss on his mouth.

Which is the exact moment when his startled gaze met mine.

And I instantly knew where I'd seen her before.

It was Miss Boobs-As-Big-As-My-Head. Her most

memorable attributes, I saw when she finally released Rob and turned around, were clothed in the skimpiest halter top imaginable.

But this time, I didn't run. This time I crossed the garage until I was standing right in front of her. Then, tilting my head so I could see into her heavily mascaraed eyes, I said, "Hi, I don't think we've met. I'm Jess, Rob's fiancée."

Boobs-As-Big-As-My-Head smiled at me in a befuddled way and said, without introducing herself, "Rob's engaged?"

"Yeah," I said. "He is. And if you ever try to kiss him like that again, I'll crack your head open with a socket wrench. Got it?"

The blonde stopped smiling.

"Oh," she said, her eyes going very wide. "Um. Yeah. I got it. I'm. Uh. I'm really sorry. I didn't know. I'm just a very affectionate person, and I tend to—"

"Well," I said with a friendly wink. "Now you do know. So knock it off."

The blonde looked questioningly at Rob, who was looking amused. And a little bit relieved.

I guess I couldn't blame him for either.

"You can pay at the counter over there, Nancy," he said. "Jake has your bill."

"Okay," Boobs-As-Big-As-My-Head said, blinking

rapidly. "Thanks again, Rob. Nice to meet you, um, Jess. And, um. I'm really sorry. Congratulations."

"Thanks. Nice meeting you," I said. "Come back soon."

On her way to the counter, Nancy nearly tripped over her own platform heels, she was in such a hurry to get away from me. I looked up at Rob, and said, "Guess what?"

"What?" he asked, still grinning.

"I'm not broken anymore," I said.

"I noticed," he said, grinning more broadly. "What happened to the whole nonviolence thing?"

"I didn't hit her," I said. "Did you see me hit her? I just threatened, is all."

"You sure did. That was some real self-restraint you exercised, as a matter of fact. So. Is it time for lunch?"

"Time for lunch."

"Just let me wash up. Hey, so the guys and I were wondering. Now that you have your powers back, does this mean if we have kids, you're always going to know where to find them?"

I thought about it. "Yes," I said.

"What about me?" He put his arms around my waist. "Are you always going to know where to find me?"

"Oh, yes," I said, grinning back at him. "Now that

I've found the person who's been missing the longest of all, anyway."

"Who's that?" Rob asked, curious.

"Myself," I said. And hugged him.

About the Author

Born in Indiana, Meg Cabot spent her childhood in pursuit of air conditioning – which she found in the public library where she spent most of her time. She has lived in California and France and currently resides in New York City with her husband and a one-eyed cat named Henrietta. Meg Cabot is the author of the hugely popular *Mediator* series as well as the bestselling *Princess Diaries*. Visit Meg at her website, www.megcabot.com

Find out how it all started . . .

MISSING

When Lightning Strikes

Jessica Mastriani has spent most of her teenage life in hot water. While other girls go cheerleading or to drama club, her extra-curricular activities include fistfights with the school football team and month-long stints in detention – luckily sitting right next to Rob, the hottest senior around.

But when Jess agrees to walk the two miles home with her best friend for a bit of exercise, she can't know that the Indiana thunderstorm brewing up around them is going to smash through her whole life and change it forever. She's struck by lightning. She lives. She's lucky. But an amazing power has been woken inside her, one that can be used for good . . . or for evil.

ISBN-10: 0-68986-091-9
ISBN-13: 978-0-68986-091-1

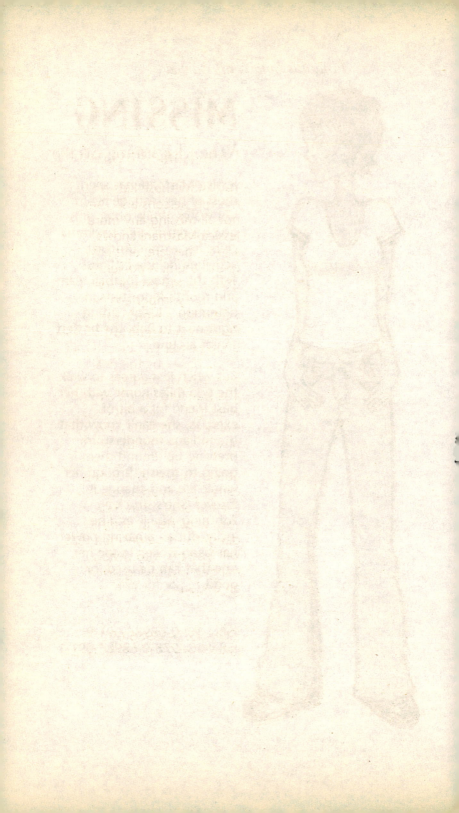

MISSING

Code Name Cassandra

You know those kids on the missing persons ad? They're not all missing any more. Jessica Mastriani knows where they are, and how to get to them. A power for good, right? Except now some very important people would like a word with Jess. People who know just how a good power can be used for evil. Chased by the police, hounded by the feds, Jess just wants to be left alone by everyone . . . except class hottie Rob Wilkins (who still hasn't called, by the way).

Stuck working at a summer camp, Jess is approached by the father of a missing girl, who begs her to find his daughter. It's a decision that will lead her into deadly danger, but saying no isn't an option . . .

ISBN-10: 0-68986-092-7
ISBN-13: 978-0-68986-092-8

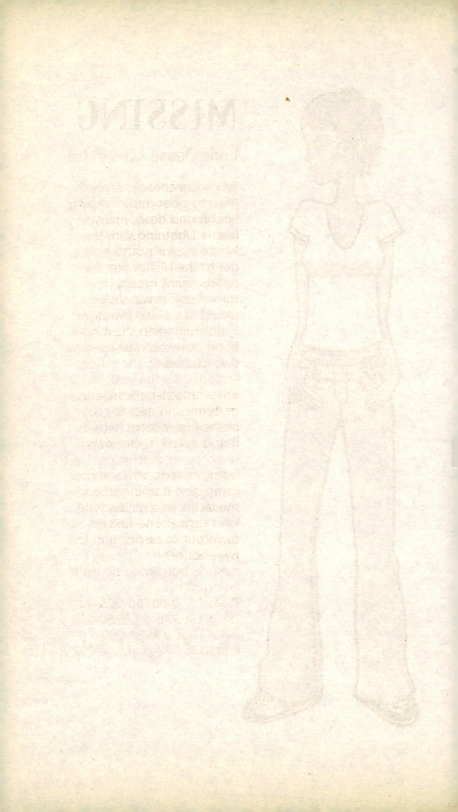

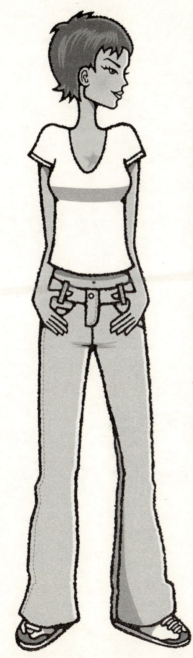

MISSING

Safe House

When cheerleader Amber Mackey goes missing and is later found dead, many blame Lightning Girl, Jess Mastriani, for not stopping the brutal killing. But when Amber went missing Jess was on holiday. It wasn't her fault! How could Jess have found her when she didn't know that she was missing in the first place?

When another cheerleader goes missing, Jess has a chance to redeem herself. But just how is she supposed to keep her psychic powers from the feds, while at the same time tracking down a murderer – especially when the number one suspect turns out to be living in Jess's own house?

ISBN-10: 0-68986-093-5
ISBN-13: 978-0-68986-093-5

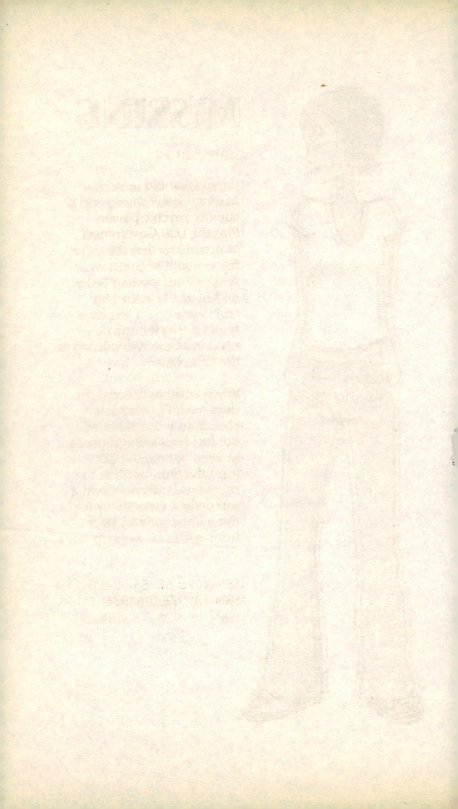

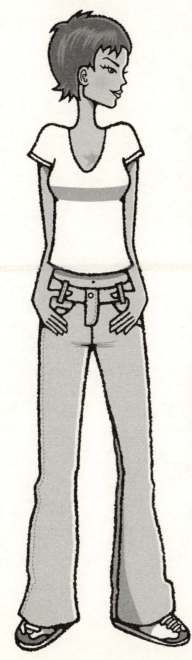

MISSING

Sanctuary

Sixteen-year-old Jess Mastriani knew she couldn't hide her psychic powers from the U.S. Government for ever. Now they want her to join a unit of 'specially gifted' crime solvers headed up by one of their agents.

However much Jess just wants to use her visions to find missing people, she's not prepared to go missing herself while on some 'classified' FBI project. But when a local boy disappears, Jess decides it's better the devil you know – anything to help find him. Can she and her would-be boyfriend Rob help unite a community and save a life – without losing their own?

ISBN-10: 0-68986-094-3
ISBN-13: 978-0-68986-094-2